DAWGS 3

THE TRIBE

SA'ID SALAAM

URBAN AESOP PUBLICATIONS

PROLOGUE

"Allahu Akbar," Arrax proclaimed and led the prayer. Harlow was in tears watching them bow and prostrate in unison. They finished and stood just as the hunter stepped from the van.

"I did it!" he announced and held up the gel tipped bullets. Their combined DNA glistened an eerie green color as it combusted and convulsed. He loaded them into the weapon just as Kenyatta and company came over the hill.

"What, the fuck?" Harlow asked as the giant beast appeared. Kenyatta was menacing enough but it was the pack of itching and twitching junkie beast with him that confused her. They were part Kenyatta but still leaning and scratching like heroin addicts. "What is this, a Thriller video?"

"Go inside!" Nandi advised and morphed into the wolf. Harlow didn't need to be told twice before rushing back into the mansion. She would watch the show from one of the many windows.

"Attack!" Kenyatta declared like the general he fancied

himself. Except his army was still leaning and nodding off the dope. They were a distraction so Nandi rushed forward and attacked. The junkies were completely helpless and she tore them to shreds. Kenyatta's army was helpless when Nandi pounced. She pulled off heads, clawed to pieces and pounced until none were left standing.

"You go low, I'll go high!" Arrax ordered just like he taught when they were kids. The hunter raised the weapon, waiting for the perfect shot. He needed the brothers just as bad as the brothers needed him. The survival of humanity hinged on this epic battle.

"I like low," Rajeem agreed and attacked. He swooped low to take a swipe but Kenyatta was faster. He swung his claws at Rajeem to remove his head. He just managed to get the blade up in time to deflect the blow.

"Argh!" Kenyatta bellowed when the plasma blade took his claws off. They could regrow in time but Arrax didn't plan on giving him any time.

"Hiyah!" he grunted and swung for Kenyatta's massive head. He managed to reel away but the blade opened his shoulder. Blood sprayed from the open wound like a sprinkler.

"If it bleeds, it can die!" Rajeem shouted and swung the blade like his samurai teacher taught him two hundred years earlier.

Arrax had been taught to wield a sword by a master British knight himself. Each

thrust, parry, poke and swipe hit paydirt. Kenyatta fought with all he had but lost some of it each time the brothers cut him. More and more wounds opened on his body, but none had the time to close. The hunter calculated the monster's recovery time until the time was right. He managed to make six bullets from the brothers DNA so they had to count. Two chops to Kenyatta's knees brought him down to size.

"Step back!" the hunter demanded as he stepped forward. Harlow crossed her fingers as the man raised the weapon. Kenyatta had the look of defeat in his eyes as he watched helplessly.

The first shot burrowed into his chest and knocked him down. The wound sizzled and smoked from the violent reaction going on inside of him. He could recover from it too if given enough time. The hunter didn't give him that time. He ran over his body and stood on his chest.

"There can be only one," he advised and fired. The bullet entered Kenyatta's head and the hunter hopped off. Just in time before his head exploded. The beast was dead, but the battle wasn't over.

"You did it! It's dead!" Arrax cheered but the hunter lifted his gun again. This time it was pointed at his chest.

"The fuck bro? We're on the same team!" Rajeem growled in human form.

"Absolutely not!" the so-called hunter snapped. "This planet is for humans! The ones God created. You, werewolves, lycans, are abominations. Predators who prey on the inhabitants of this world! Meet markets! Breeding centers!"

"It was you! Qatar? Yemen?" Arrax finally understood. It was him who was killing his kind and werewolves around the globe.

"What, exactly, are you supposed to be?" Rajeem asked and sniffed once more to be sure. He almost smelled human but there was something more to him. Something he couldn't make out.

"I'm complicated. I am Martin Jones. Son of Martin Jones, the Dark Prince," he said and fired. Rajeem rushed in front of his brother and took the round meant for him. The impact sent them both sprawling to the ground.

"Arrax!" Harlow shouted from the window when her man went down.

"Stay inside!" Nandi demanded and morphed once more.

"Are you OK?" Arrax asked his brother on top of him but Rajeem was too dead to reply. A large hole went straight through his body. He sprang to his feet and quickly transformed. Martin was just as quick with the weapon and fired again.

The first shot spun Arrax around where a second shot met him. This one dropped him as Nandi sprang into the air. The hunter fired and knocked her right out of the sky. She fell dead on top of the only love she ever knew. Arrax managed to turn his head and lock eyes with his own love. A soft smile spread as he welcomed a long overdue death. He never wanted to live forever and was ready to be reunited with his loved ones who went before him. He died with that same smile on his face.

"Wait!" Harlow screamed as she came out of the mansion. The hunter stopped and tilted his head curiously. Surely she didn't want to fight him too. That's exactly what she wanted though. She stuck out her chest and demanded death. "Don't just leave me! You just killed everyone I love! Kill me too!"

"I only kill monsters. Werewolves, lycans and vampires. There can be only one," Martin said and turned. "I am the one."

CHAPTER 1

"No baby, no," Harlow moaned as she cradled Arrax's head in her lap. She had to share her mourning between the love of her life and her long lost sister laying nearby.

Nandi was sprawled on top of the only love she ever had.

All she could do was stare off in the direction Martin left after taking everything from her. After a lifetime of looking for love in all the wrong men. Another lifetime searching for her baby sister. She finally had it all, then it was all taken away in an instant.

"I have nothing to live for," she decided. Her decision was made so the tears stopped falling down her pretty brown face.

The pistol she packed in her purse was worthless against the monsters but she was very mortal. She pulled and made sure a round was in the chamber. She only had one pull of the trigger in her so she had to get it right. A final kiss to her lover's lips and she lifted the gun to her temple.

"See you in a sec babe..." Harlow sighed and squeezed the trigger. She heard the shot before registering the hand that moved the barrel away from her head. It took a few blinks of disbelief to believe what she was seeing. She was looking down at Arrax looking up at her. The hole in his chest closed and made him gasp.

"What happened?" Arrax asked as the events came rushing back to him. He popped up and looked over to his brother. Just as Rajeem's legs began to twitch. His eyes came open just before his mouth.

"Get off me girl!" Rajeem fussed and nudged his woman.

"You weren't saying that a few minutes ago," Nandi sassed as she stood. Her mind flashed back to the blast that killed her and she looked down for the hole.

"Oh my god!" You're alive! All of you are alive!" Harlow shrieked and squeezed her man. A second thought released him a second later and she rushed over to her sister.

"This chick's gonna kill me again!" Nandi laughed as her sister squeezed her tightly. That gave the brothers a chance to climb to their feet and speak.

"I saw my place in the hell fire," Rajeem said with the awe a sight like that would inspire. "There were valleys of fire. Boiling water, the screams."

"The screams," Arrax nodded since he saw it as well. He could hear the roar of the fire as if it were breathing. "There was a tree, the fruits were like the heads of devils."

"I saw that! My skin, it burned off. Then grew right back and burned again!" Nandi said as she rushed over to her man. She too had seen the violent fire while in between this life and the next. "What does that mean?"

"Means we have a second chance," Rajeem replied but looked over to his brother for confirmation.

"Possibly," Arrax replied because people will see their place in the hell fire and beg to be returned so they can do good. Only to fall right back into the same pattern that doomed them in the first place. His chest instinctively stuck out on it's own to match his determination to not be one of those people.

"We're not going to see ummi," Rajeem moaned when it dawned on him. Their mother was a devout Muslimah as wasn't where they were headed.

"Yes we are!" Arrax insisted. He sounded a lot more confident than he felt. He had the right idea but no plan on what to do next. His eyes traveled over to the remnants of Kenyatta and his junkie army and pushed a sigh from his chest. "He's right, you know."

"The prince guy, Martin. Yeah, he was. We don't belong here," Rajeem caught on since he wondered the same. He had caused corruption on these people's earth for hundreds of years. This was their planet, they were uninvited guests. Nandi's eyes went wide at the mention of the name that sent her to hell. She looked in every direction, hoping not to see him in any.

"Maybe," Arrax guessed, even though he knew his brother was right about Martin's being right. Dude had just killed them so he wasn't too keen on giving him props at the moment. Plus, there were other matters pressing. "I feel, different?"

"Me too?" Rajeem admitted. He felt whatever it was since coming back to life, but wouldn't have spoken up if Arrax hadn't. Yet again there were more pressing matters to tend.

"Let's get out of here," Arrax suggested but stopped short of naming a destination. The Dark Prince seemed to know their moves before they made it so where could they go.

Another issue gnawed at him like a young wolf determined to reach the creamy marrow inside a bone. Something was missing. The what, is what he needed to figure out.

"Roman's," Harlow suggested since she felt somewhat safe in the fortress.

"Yeah, no. Nothing left of it" he sighed and shook his head. They still had to leave this crime scene so he turned and led the way from the park.

"Cool!" Harlow cheered when they reached the electric motorcycles. Rajeem wanted to gloat over them but the loss of Harold wouldn't let him. He had a guy and got him killed.

The women climbed behind their men as the bikes hummed to life. The vibration from the powerful motor beneath eased their minds as they fled the crime scene. Arrax pondered over one of many dilemmas and pulled to a stop. Everything was left behind and they needed cash to go forward.

He tacitly explained by walking up to an ATM machine and punching through with his bare hand. Rajeem nodded in approval as he came out with stacks of cash in each hand. Once he remounted the bike they headed back towards the airport.

Everyone hoped but no one spoke on whether or not the Dark Prince could or would be in the airport. By their calculations he still had at least one more of the bullets that could kill them. Which once again made Arrax wonder why he didn't. They would figure that out once they got where they were going. The rest found out where that was when they reached the ticket counter.

"England?" Harlow repeated when he purchased four first class tickets.

"I have a home there," he explained but was no closer to

explaining what was eating at him. The group silently made their way through the airport and boarded the plane. There wasn't much to say until the plane reached cruising altitude.

"Well, we died so..." Rajeem said as he stood. Nandi accepted his hand and stood with him. She wiggled her eyes at her sister and followed her man.

"Just nasty," Harlow laughed as they headed towards the bathroom. Which were a lot roomier here in the first class.

"Hold that thought," Arrax added since he was feeling the same way. Seeing his place in the hell fire made him want to enjoy life until he died. He also needed to live life right while he could. This was a second chance, so maybe he didn't have to go to hell. "We're getting married when we land."

"Are we? So, you're not even going to ask huh?" Harlow huffed in faux indignation.

"No," he said and leaned back. His body took it's right and drifted to sleep as the Atlantic ocean passed beneath them.

"Oh, OK then," she told the sleeping man and went to sleep on his shoulder.

"Jolly ole England!" Rajeem announced as they headed through Heathrow airport
. "I haven't been in since..."

"Nineteen seventy eight!" Arrax quickly helped out. His brother may have forgotten but no way he could after all the chaos Rajeem and a band of werewolves caused.

"Oh yeah..." he laughed and recalled the fond memories of murder and mayhem. Somehow it brought him right back to his recent death.

He vividly recalled being in the state of the grave when

two angels came to question him. They asked who was his Lord. What was his religion and who was his prophet? Once upon a time he knew those answers but now only 'ah, ah, ah' came to mind. "Allah. Islam, Muhammad..."

"I forgot as well," Arrax admitted

when he heard the answers he had forgotten as well. Those same angels came and posed the same question in death. The sisters weren't sure what put the faraway looks on their men's faces. They huddled together and followed out to the line of taxis. He gave the driver the address in Kensington as they piled in.

"Figures your bougie ass would live there," Rajeem laughed

when they reached one of the high rent districts in the city.

"And I bet you prefer Hackney?" he shot back without denying being bougie. Not that he could since had become quite bougie over the centuries.

"Yes sir!" he agreed while Harlow and Nandi looked between them. The sisters had never been to London and didn't know the difference. Part of Rajeem's enthusiasm came from the variety of vaginas the area contained. He couldn't share that now with Nandi present. Having a woman is a lot different than just, having a woman. Nandi was his woman and he was content.

"Wow, this is nice!" Harlow cheered when they reached the high rise building.

"Huh? Yeah, thanks," Arrax replied and used his super sense of scent to determine if there would be a problem. He had walked out on his ex over a year ago and didn't know if she stayed or left. No trace of her scent remained which meant she left shortly after he did. Arrax didn't have an extra key but he was extra strong so the lock and door eagerly spread for him like those women Rajeem liked in Hackney.

"You guys are over there," he said pointing to the spare bedroom. It had been a long day followed by a long flight. He was asleep before his head hit the pillow.

"Mmhm," Harlow hummed down him. She had some fussing to do but it would have to wait.

CHAPTER 2

"What the..." Arrax reeled when his eyes opened the next morning and found two eyes bearing down at him.

"Mmhm," Harlow hummed from the same position from the night before. She had caught a few hours of sleep and got back to her station. Determined to have her way.

"No," he said animatedly and shook his head, before rolling out of bed and into the bathroom. He hoped to relieve his bladder in peace but there was Harlow right at his side.

"Mmhm!" she hummed again to his shaking head. A head shake can mean no, but she wasn't taken no for an answer. "You promised to turn me! Once this was over and it's over."

"Something tells me this is far from over," he said more to himself than her. Everything about life was different after returning from the dead.

"All I know is y'all were dead and I was left alone!" she fussed.

"You were left alive, you mean!" Arrax shot back. "There's

a war on our kind. On all supernatural beings. A war we can't win. We won't win."

"Then I'll die with my loved ones

. We're a team. A tribe! We should live, or die, together." Harlow insisted. "Now, I can be lycan like you, or wolf like them."

"My brother..." Arrax began until it dawned on him that her sister could and most likely would turn her. He could ask Rajeem not to but not Nandi. "OK. You win."

"Yay!" Harlow cheered and spun around in the bathroom. She did a pop lock and passed the arm wave to Arrax who just shook his head again.

"Let's see how 'yay' this is..." Arrax said and began to morph. Harlow closed her eyes and tensed for the bite.

Arrax felt the increase in his own size but it was confirmed when he crushed the light fixture above his head. He was crouched over to fit under the nine foot ceilings. Something had changed but he still bit into her shoulder. The feel of bone was the limit and he let his supernatural saliva mix with her mortal blood.

"Ssss!" Harlow hissed and winced through the pain. She lifted her chin in confidence, then died.

Arrax had to bend even further to look at himself in the mirror. He was larger and hairier but the changes went beyond looks. He felt, sensed and smelled different than ever. It was more than he intended to deal with at the moment so he shrank back to his human form and left the room.

"Good morning bro," Rajeem greeted when Arrax entered the front room.

"Yeah, I heard," he chuckled as the sounds of their love making rang through the flat that morning. Nandi blushed under her melanin and looked behind him for her sister.

"Where's Harlow?" she asked when she didn't appear after him.

"Dead," Arrax said, pointing with his head.

"Yay!" Nandi cheered and did the same spin and dance her sister had done. The same one they did as girls back in Ohio. The brothers laughed and stepped out on the terrace.

"That shot did something to us," Arrax said and nodded at the fact.

"I thought so! My dick seems bigger than ever!" Rajeem exclaimed. He laughed at his own joke but he was definitely different. He felt more powerful even now, even though he had yet to morph. Even Nandi felt the difference.

"From my DNA. I got yours as well," Arrax ascertained. "I hope that doesn't mean my dick will shrink!"

"Wouldn't shrink much!" he laughed. The laughter died soon and seriousness swept back over them. "Had to be the shot!"

"And he had to know that," Arrax said and titled his head at the raven that landed on the railing. "He could have killed us. Why did he keep us alive?"

"I..." Rajeem opened his mouth to answer the question he couldn't answer but the bird spoke up first.

"Because I need you," it said before landing on the floor and growing into a man. The brothers blinked as the Dark Prince appeared before them. The sound of furniture breaking turned heads to see Nandi transforming to face the threat.

"Wait!" Rajeem ordered before she could attack. Even she felt her new size and the new power coursing through her. Her fangs were nearly twice as long as ever.

"Down girl!" the Dark Prince laughed and turned back to the men. "This world is for humans."

"Bruh, you are not human!" Arrax insisted. An easy call

since he was just a talking crow. That was cool but Rajeem had questions.

"What did you do to us?" he needed to know as the giant she wolf in the next room shrank back to human form. A naked human form that caught the man's attention until she ducked into the bedroom.

"Why didn't it kill us?" Arrax added.

"If I wanted you dead, you would be. Dead," he assured them both. "You share a parent so your DNA stabilizes. Kenyatta did not so it killed him. As it kills most monsters."

"And since I turned her..." Rajeem opined and nodded the man's head again.

"You became part of her, so it didn't harm her as well. It did effectively cross breed the two species. You now share the same strengths but none of the same weaknesses," the Dark Prince relayed. A smile spread on his face when he caught the tacit conversation the brothers held with a glance. "I can read minds, you know? To answer your question, I can destroy you whenever I like!"

"Then why didn't you?" Rajeem snarled and slowly morphed his face and mouth. Arrax let his claws slowly expand.

"Damit..." Nandi said at the thought of shredding another outfit since she was about to morph again and join the fray after just changing clothes.

"Like I said..." he began, then disappeared in a puff of smoke. Only to reappear a second later behind them. "I want your help. Or, you can die."

"What's to stop you from killing us after we help you?" Arrax asked and retracted his claws.

"Because you want to live. Live as mortals. My mother perfected the formula to reverse the species. Everyone refused, so they died," he informed.

Arrax just blinked at the thought of being mortal again. Having children, catching a cold, sneezing. Even dying a mortal death had appeal after seeing his place in the hell fire. He longed to see his parents in the afterlife but he was headed in the wrong direction.

"Why don't you take it? You're not human!" Rajeem said, still stuck between species. Nandi too waited to see which way this would go.

"I have the cure. Now, I'm going to finish what I started. You can join me and live, or..." Martin said and let them finish the thought. There were still thousands of werewolves, lycans and vampires around the globe. Their ability to turn others had them multiplying like rabbits. Quicker than he could handle on his own.

"Why..." Arrax began to ask but the man turned into a bird and the bird took flight before he reached the, "Us?"

"Why not us!" Rajeem cheered. "We were good once! Well, you more than me, but ummi raised us right! To be good!"

"She did. We were, we could be," Arrax processed. They retreated back inside and Nandi rushed over to lock the door behind them. Not that a lock could stop the most powerful vampire on the planet. Martin Jones wasn't turned though, he was born this way...

"Turn your head!" Melcina warned when the earth shook beneath them as they rode from the showdown in the park. She had been trained for this day in hope it never came.

"Mommy, daddy," young Martin moaned as his parents' life force went silent in an instant. Black babies have been surviving off one parent ever since the master showed black men how to knock up black women and turn their back.

They learned well and abandoned their kids like it was commendable instead of abominable.

Black kids still excelled with one parent in spite of the odds against them. Martin now had no parents and was left with the nanny to raise him. Sure she had instructions but what good are instructions without someone to ensure they are followed.

"I know baby," Melcina purred and rubbed his curly head. It may have sounded convincing to the cab driver but Martin could read minds. He couldn't manage the many mixed thoughts and questions swirling around her head. The rest of the ride was made in silence until they reached the Bronx high rise building.

"Here?" Melcina asked since she had never been here before.It seemed like another planet from the swank neighborhood they lived in. Only because it was.

"A 'huned sixty six and Ogden. That's what you said," the driver reminded and looked at the meter. "Gotta add twenty bucks to it for crossing the bridge."

"Liar. You just want a crack to smoke!" Martin fussed up at him. He could read minds even if he was too young to decipher what things meant. He turned to his nanny and asked, "What's a crack?"

"Something he won't get with our money!" she spat and paid exactly what was on the meter. She got out and looked up at the massive concrete structure that would be their new home for a while. Two keys were tucked into a compartment in her purse but she never thought the day would come that she had to use it.

Martin looked up and around at all the new faces looking at his and her new faces. She used the key with the word 'lobby' and let them both in. The next key had the number and letter 16-h, so they caught the elevator up to the sixteenth floor.

"H!" Martin said pointing at the first door on the left when they exited.

"H it is," she sighed and stuck the key into the lock. She had no idea what to expect on the other side but would have never guessed this.

"It's just like at home!" Martin exclaimed and rushed inside. He spun, looked around and confirmed, "It's just like home!"

"It is?" she replied, bewildered. With good reason since the apartment was furnished exactly like the one downtown. The only differences were in the layout but everything there was here.

"My toys are here!" Martin called from the back. That prompted Melcina to check what would be her room and sure enough, duplicates of everything she had was tucked away here.

The multi million dollar apartment back over in Manhattan was smoldering from the self destruct mechanism Kristine set up in case they met their demise. When the system no longer registered her and Martin's heartbeats it began the fire that destroyed any traces of her research. Only in the apartment though because duplicates of all her files, research and formulas were tucked away for a later time.

"Play me," Martin read aloud and took the DVD into the living room to his guardian. Melcina kept her thoughts in check and loaded the disk. A stoic Mr and Mrs Jones stared straight ahead into the camera.

"My dear son. If you are watching, that means we are no more," Kristine began but her husband cut in.

"Dead son. She means dead," Martin Sr explained. "No more, sounds like cookies. No more cookies."

"Can I do this?" she fussed and turned back to the camera. "My dear boy, this is what has been written for you. For us, so don't worry. Everything will remain the same. Melcina will take good care of you. She will ask you to bite her, one day. Don't! Promise me."

"I promise mommy!" he vowed during the pause his mother left for him to do so. A smile spread on her face as if she could hear him. She must have seen the look on the nanny's face and turned to her.

"Melcina. You too, will be well taken care of. He has a trust fund set up for his twenty-first birthday. As do you. We will be with you every step of the way. You must follow our directions to the letter. Do you understand?" Kristine asked, peering through the screen from the afterlife.

"Yes?" Melcina nodded as if the woman could see. Her piercing gaze made her wonder if the woman couldn't see them. Lord knows she had seen the Jones' do some remarkable things. Raising their child from beyond the grave would be added to that list.

"Good. The card on your dresser has our lawyer's information. Call him. He will make sure you have everything you need to raise him as we want him raised."

"Yes ma'am," Melcina nodded in agreement. She and Martin would watch that video message five more times that day. It was all they had left of the loving couple, for now. She had many questions she wouldn't ask. He had only one and no kid ever shied away from asking anything.

"Why would I bite you?" he wondered and scrunched his face.

"I mean, only if I bit you. Then you could bite me back," Melcina replied and nodded to make it true. She kept her motive ulterior so he wouldn't pick it from her brain. Martin wasn't sure if he should agree or not. He had been taught by his dad to hit back when hit so it made sense to bite back if bit. However his mother clearly told him not to bite her.

"Mommy said no!" he said adamantly and shook his head. Not that Melcina would give up since she longed for the powers she once had as a vampire.

He had no idea what a bite from the most powerful hybrid vampire on the planet would do. Neither did she.

CHAPTER 3

Melcina followed the directions and called the lawyer. He instructed her to come to his office the following day to collect the bank cards and other paperwork to care for the boy. They almost forgot their new surroundings since the interior was so similar. That all went out the window when they walked out the door.

"There he is!" a young teen cheered when Melcina and Martin appeared from the building that would be their new home. He was older than Martin by years but still spotted the new Jordan's on his feet when they came in. The only J's he knew was his junkie mother and aunts so he stole everything he saw.

"Here," Martin said naively as the kid approached with two flunkies flanking him. Melcina tilted her head curiously as the boy reached down to remove his sneakers.

"What are you doing?" she wondered and looked between him and the teens.

"He wants my sneakers," little Martin explained since it was the only thing on the teens mind. Martin could even see his intentions to buy a turkey and cheese hero once he sold them.

"Well, he's not getting them! Get up!" she demanded of him and turned to them. "He's not giving you anything! Not now, not ever!"

"He ain't gotta give. This Highbridge, we take!" he said and swooped down to take the shoes himself. Martin just blinked when Melcina shoved him away. His face changed when he read the dangerous thoughts that followed. He knew the knife was coming out before he pulled it.

"Now, I'm taking err thing!" the teen declared and flicked the 007 knife open.

"No!" Martin said and moved so quickly no one saw him. All they saw was the knife was now in his hand.

"Gimme that!" Melcina demanded and snatched it away. She put it between herself and the would-be robbers. "Come on!"

"You got that," the boy backed away with his hands up. She knew he would be a problem from now on. She also knew Martin could help her, help them.

"Mommy said no," Martin whined when her thoughts screamed 'bite me!' in his head.

"That's rude! It's not nice to read my thoughts!" she huffed and tuned out so there would be nothing to read. Her hand raised to hail a gypsy cab rambling down Ogden avenue. "A hundred and sixty first street!"

"OK mama," the driver agreed and watched her through the mirror.

"Ewww!" Martin grimaced and Melcina cracked up. She didn't need to read minds to know what the driver was thinking as he looked her up and down.

"Good for you! Stop being nosey!" she laughed. Martin had the ability to turn it off so that's exactly what he did. He had enough to think about wondering why the man wanted to lick her private parts.

"Mr Walsh will see you now!" the pretty receptionist sang and smiled. Martin got a wink with his smile and giggled.

"Thank you," Melcina said and sighed. This whole corporate life scared her and left her feeling out of place. Still, she followed the woman and entered the corner office.

"Melcina! I heard a lot about you!" Mr Walsh said and rushed from behind his desk to shake their hands.

"You have?" she wondered since she was simply a simple nanny in her own mind. She had written herself off and those are the hardest obstacles to overcome.

"Yes! The Jones' spoke very highly of you!" he assured her before turning to him. "Nice to see you again Martin."

"Yes sir," he nodded and shook his large hand. Melcina helped him into one of the chairs in front of his desk and they got down to business.

Luckily for her, the little boy had an extremely high IQ and photographic memory. He both understood and retained every word spoken while she nodded along to things that went over her head. Mr and Mrs Jones had prepared well for this inevitability. They didn't have any life insurance policies to sort through but did leave millions behind. Their finances were highly structured so no one could take a dime.

"Mrs Kristine said something about a trust fund?" Melcina asked after receiving the debit and credit cards.

"Yes. Martin will receive a sum at eighteen and the bulk of his parents estate at age twenty one. You'll receive a million dollar payout on that same day," he replied and watched her eyes do exactly what he expected to do.

Kristine and Martin trusted her but also knew people work better when there is something in it for them. A million somethings was plenty to do what she would have done anyway.

"Um," she asked and raised her hand to ask a question. He nodded so she put it out there. "Can we move? We don't like that area!"

"No. Martin insisted he stays there!" Mr Walsh quickly interjected. He took his clients' wishes very seriously even if he didn't understand them. This was one wish he did understand quite well since his humble beginnings began in the jungle of South Jamaica Queens. "The rough neighborhood will prepare him for life has in store."

"Here we go again!" Melcina groaned when she saw the same group of kids out in front of the building when they returned. She assumed they were waiting on them but she was wrong. Those kids hanging out in front of that building would one day be adults hanging out in front of that building.

"Don't worry," Martin said and took her hand. Comfort swept through her from his touch and the worry went away. He didn't understand he had the power to make people do what he wanted them to do.

"You coming off them J's now!" the same kid declared as he led a larger pack towards them. They all had stick-ball sticks in hand but no ball. Martin looked at one of the other boys who stopped in his tracks. He nodded and caught up with the rest just as they reached their victims.

"Q?" he called to the leader and began to swing the stick. He knocked the 'huh' from his mouth along with a front tooth.

"Fuck you do that for Ant-man!" another of the crew asked but got whacked for an answer. He turned his stick on the rest of his friends while Martin and Melcina walked by and entered the building. Ant-man swung ferociously to defend Martin and Melcina.

"How did you do that?" Melcina wanted to know. Even during her stint as a vampire she couldn't control minds. That was a power that had to be honed over the ages. Martin just shrugged since he was born with it. She could only shake her head and lean in to bite his arm playfully. "Grrrr!"

"Nope!" Martin laughed and didn't bite her back. He did bite into his dinner before bath time followed closely by bedtime. His parents insisted he start his new school right away.

The large high rise they now lived in had the elementary school built into the side of it. They billed it as a convenience but didn't say to whom. Keeping these hood kids in their hood made it convenient for the city to keep tabs on them.

They awoke bright and early the next morning and prepared for school just like they had a few days ago when he had parents. Their plan to keep life as close to normal seemed to be working for now. His busy schedule would keep his mind too occupied to dwell on his losses.

Melcina was on high alert when they exited the building but the thugs were nowhere in sight. Except for Ant-man and his stick. He was still wearing the same clothes since he had been there all night. Ant-man nodded at Martin who nodded back to relieve him of duty.

"Grrr," she laughed and bit his shoulder through his shirt. He laughed along with her even though she was very serious.

Mortal life sucked after experiencing the supernatural life of a vampire.

"Well hello Mr Jones!" the new teacher sang when they reached the class. Martin looked around since the only Mr Jones he knew was his dad.

"She means you," Melcina laughed.

"Oh, hello," he replied and followed her inside. Martin became the smartest kid in class as soon as he stepped in the room. He would breeze through class, the grade and grade school.

By age sixteen Martin Jones Jr was as tall and handsome as his father. The same smooth chocolate skin tone and deep, dark eyes had a hypnotic effect on people. He still hadn't discovered his hidden powers but people flocked to him like a rock star.

Some of those good looks came from his good looking mother but he had all of her brain power. Thanks to yearly videos released by his parents his mother steered him in the field of science. Thanks in part to her posthumous tutelage he was a senior in the prestigious Bronx High School of Science at sixteen years old.

Kristine was grooming the boy in her way but his father was doing the same. Each yearly video introduced him to a new art and teacher of self defense. He was a black belt in karate, judo, jujitsu as well as a beast of a brawler in a mixed martial arts cage.

He never had to use his formidable skills since Ant-man, Q and the others from his building followed him like an entourage. They were now grown but would escort him to and from school everyday. Melcina once asked why they did it but no one could answer. Martin had the power to control weak minds like a chess master.

"Your parents must be rappers or something?" a pretty little blonde suggested when Martin was dropped off at school by his hoodlum security detail.

"Why do you say that?" he asked instead of peering inside her head for the answer. Something he had sworn off once getting a taste of the malice that lingers behind most smiles.

"Well, you're rich, and you have security," she shot back since the only rich black people she ever saw were rappers.

"My parents are deceased," he sighed without admitting that his father was indeed a super star rapper.

"My bad. You do kinda look like the old school rapper, Dark Prince. My mom says she met him at a show a long time ago," she said.

"He was my dad," Martin relayed. Neither knew her mother was just one of many groupies who gave the late rapper some head after a show. History would repeat itself when she gave Martin some head after history class.

He didn't need his mind to control vaginas. His good looks and nice clothes did that for him.

CHAPTER 4

"You look nice!" Martin cheered when Melcina emerged from the bathroom.

"I sure do!" she agreed and did a twirl. At sixteen Martin was plenty old enough to watch himself while she went for a night on the town. With all the girls chasing behind him, he was getting more action than her.

In fact, she hadn't had any since before Mr and Mrs Jones departed this earth. Still, that wasn't what was driving her tonight. She never gave up on her quest to become a vampire again. The Jones had knocked a serious dent in the vampire population but they were slowly coming back.

Her research led her to several underground clubs rumored to have vampires. Most didn't pan out and turned out to be more than wannabes and make believers, pretending to be vampires. Drinking kool aid and red bull instead of blood. The power and excitement fueled her on, so off she went.

"No girls while I'm gone!" Melcina warned sternly over her shoulder as she left.

"No girls," he agreed and made a call to the grown woman he had been seeing on the twenty first floor.

"Broadway," Melcina told the driver as soon as she sat inside. He turned to complain about the one way fare since no one on Broadway would be coming back to the Bronx. The two hundred dollar bills that met him and silenced his gripes.

"Broadway it is!" he cheered and pulled off. He had made more than the meter would read so he didn't bother to turn it on. "Hitting the club?"

"Unless you hit a pole and kill us!" she shot back since he was looking more at her legs through the mirror than the street through the windshield.

"I got this ma!" he laughed and managed to alternate between the city streets and her brown legs all the way downtown.

"There!" she said triumphantly when she spotted a red light above a door.

"Here?" he asked unsurely since he couldn't see the sign she saw. It had no formal signage, except the small red light. Even the block looked deserted and he was leery about leaving her.

"Here!" she said eagerly. The trace amounts of vampire in her cells tingled, letting her know she was in the right place. There was a vampire somewhere close.

"Want I should wait for you?" he asked. Not just for the return fare but something made the hairs on his arms stand.

"No. Yes, no. Give me your number," she decided after a brief bout of vacillation. It would be nearly impossible to catch a taxi back uptown and the subway was just ghetto as far as she was concerned.

"Here," he laughed and handed the card over while

stealing another glance at her legs. She took the card and exited the car. "I'll just wait."

Melcina took in a deep breath and exhaled a 'here we go' sigh. Martin would never disobey his mother so there was zero chance of him turning her. This was her chance, so she stuck her chest out and stepped up to the door.

"Yeah?" a voice replied to the tapping that hurt her knuckles. She looked down at this same hand that could once punch through a cinder block. Now it hurts just from knocking on a door. All of that instead of answering the voice so a slide slid open to reveal a pair of bloodshot eyes. "Can't hear? I said yeah!"

"I hear just fine," Melcina shot back with some salt, then turned to the sugar. "Hey handsome. Is this The Spot?"

The eyes narrowed but she was here and did know the little known name. The shoulders shrugged followed by the clicks and clacks of multiple locks being unlocked. Followed by a heavy bar being lifted and finally the door opened.

"Thank you sir..." Melcina was saying until realizing he was a she. "I mean, ma'am."

"Oh, I was handsome just a minute ago," she chided minus any mirth. She stepped aside and nodded at the next door, vibrating from the thundering music on the other side.

"Thanks," she said and stepped inside. The sweet, coppery smell of blood mingled with the cologne and perfume from both sexes as well as the sex, smoke and danger hovering in the air. She inhaled deeply and knew this was indeed the spot.

Melcina danced her way to the middle of the dancefloor and let her ample hips sway to the music. It wasn't long until a male body pressed against her from behind. He held her hips and let her grind on his crotch until he had a full fledged erection.

"Mmmm," she moaned and grinded even harder. Harder, making him harder, then faster until she made him moan. The man went stiff when he bust a nut in his slacks. He had an extra hundred dollar bill tucked away in his wallet for a nut like this and now it looked like he could keep it.

"Mortal!" Melcina huffed and twisted her lips as she left him shivering in the middle of the dancefloor. Vampires don't come that quick so she knew he was human. She reached the bar for a drink and looked up at a table in the rear. Her eyes found a pair looking back at hers and locked in.

"What can I get you?" the bartender asked as she turned away.

"Nothing. I found what I'm looking for..." she said to herself since he couldn't hear her. Melcina marched over to the table and took a seat. Her cells tingled even more in his presence. He was nowhere as strong as Martin and Kristine but he was definitely a vampire.

"What do you want?" he asked and peered into her soul like vampires do. He still had work to do with his hypnotics and cracked her up.

"I want what I had!" she cheered even though she knew he wouldn't understand. "I want you, to turn me! But first..."

The but first was more of a butt, first since she reached for his zipper and freed his dick from the tight pants. She stuck her tongue in her mouth and tugged on his dick until it grew long and hard in her hand. Her wet panties easily slid to the side as she mounted his lap right there at the table.

"Shit!" they both fussed for similar reasons. For her it was having a man inside her again after over a decade of no dick. It was the tightness for him. Most easy pussy like this was loose as goose but it was tight as a glove.

"Do it!" she dared as he ran his tongue on her jugular vein.

He could literally taste the sweet blood through her skin. His fangs slid from his gums as she thrusted her hips in a circle. A mix of ecstasy and pain lolled her head back as he penetrated her neck.

The vampire held on as her blood rushed into his mouth. He fought the urge to suck like a child with a juice pack, and let his saliva mix with her blood. Her hips kept on gyrating and he interjected another bodily fluid as he ejaculated inside of her. No, Vampires don't generally come that quick but chicks don't usually work their hips like that either.

"Ahhhhh!" both groaned at the same time, yet for different reasons. She got a good nut and could feel his saliva coursing through her body.

"Thanks," Melcina thanked and got off his lap. She pulled her panties back in place since what goes up will come down. She rushed from the club and saw the same car that dropped her. Mark had taken a break to smoke a joint since he was ahead of the game.

"Hey!" he greeted happily when she tapped on the window. "Get up front!"

"Thanks! Can you hurry, please?" she asked, then answered her own question with two more hundred dollar bills.

"Sure can, for you ma!" he cheered and cheesed as he accepted the money. He got an added tip since he was able to get a closer look at those legs since she was sitting up front with her.

Melcina yawned to fight what she knew was coming. Her eyes closed and she leaned back, trying to hold it off as long as possible. The closed eyes were a green light for Mark. He started off timidly touching her knee. Then gave her soft thigh a squeeze that made his dick hard. His hand inched under her dress as he sped uptown.

"Pussy all wet!" he cheered like the home team scored a touchdown when he finally reached her crotch. He pulled those same panties aside and fondled her box. It was slippery wet on his fingers so he slid one inside.

His head shook away the idea of pulling over and taking some pussy. He did manage to get his dick out though. Mark kept the vehicle straight with his knees and scooped some of the wetness from between her legs to use as a lube. Now he multitasked by fondling her pussy, jacking his dick and driving the car at the same time.

It wasn't long until he blew his load on the steering wheel, dashboard and his pants. They had crossed over the hundred and fifty ninth street bridge when he finally pulled his hand from her box. He had no intention of letting all that wetness go to waste either so he sucked his fingers dry.

"Mm-mm," he moaned but only because he didn't know it was vampire nut he was tasting.

"Hmp!" she huffed since she felt the whole episode with her eyes closed.

"Call me when you need me again!" Mark said as he crossed over one hundred and sixty fifth street and stopped where he got her.

"I sure will," Melcina managed and stumbled out of the vehicle. She staggered up the walk and into the building. Even mortal kids can hear their parents keys in the elevator before they get home but Martin could smell and sense her as she walked through the lobby. By the time the elevator reached their floor he was fake snoring loud enough to be heard from the hallway.

"Mmhm," Melcina said as she stumbled into her room and onto her bed. She let out a sigh of relief and died right there on the spot.

CHAPTER 5

"Hmmm?" Martin hummed the next morning. Melcina was usually awake and breakfast was usually made. She was paid well but did those things out of love for him.

He exited his room and looked down the hall at the closed bedroom door. An eerie feeling swept through him but he wasn't ready for eerie this early. Instead he headed to the kitchen to fix his own breakfast. Saturday was as busy as a Monday in the life of this busy boy. His parents still raised him from the grave as they would if they were still alive.

A thick steak was perfectly thawed and seasoned in the fridge. Martin had seen his mother and then Melcina cook enough to figure his way through a steak and egg breakfast. It wasn't quite like theirs but not bad either. Enough protein and calories to handle his first assignment of the day.

"Here he comes!" Q announced to Ant-man when he saw Martin getting off the elevator. Both knew his schedule enough to be out front when he came out. Neither knew why they were so devoted to him because the weak minds are the easiest to control.

Martin still didn't grasp his ability to control people's minds. He was still naive enough to think it was a coincidence that people just happened to do what he wanted them to do. He only had to wish the local thugs protected him instead of harassing him and they had been protecting him ever since.

"Hey Prince!" Ant-man cheered. Like it or not he had adopted his late father's moniker along with the face.

"Sup guys. Hungry?" Martin asked and handed each a steak biscuit. Another way he controlled hearts and minds was through his generosity. Some parts of the Bronx are third world countries. Highbridge was some parts. Food goes a long way in third world countries.

"Hells yeah!" Ant-man proclaimed. They scarfed down their meals as they headed down to 161st street to catch the train.

Martin had enough money to take a taxi all the way downtown instead of walking down the hill, to the train and riding downtown. This was more adventurous and the sights were certainly better. Especially one sight in particular that he particularly liked to see.

"There she goes, Prince!" Q reported since his leader was looking in the wrong direction. Prince had been watching the windows and door of a tenement building hoping for a glimpse of the beautiful Puerto Rican teen, but she had just stepped from the bodega across the street.

"Buenos dias bonita," Prince said in pitch perfect Spanish. Just one of several languages his deceased mother had him master.

"Good morning," Ximena replied with a coy smile and eye flutter. Then rushed inside her building as her mother peered down from her window. Her modesty turned him on even more than the plump breast and fat ass she tried to conceal in oversized clothes. A far cry from the fast teens who kept the thirsty young man satisfied.

"She likes you Prince!" Ant-man assured him.

"She not fucking tho! Won't give nobody no pussy!" Q lambasted as if the hood had a right to her vagina. It's a crazy world when keeping one's pubic area private is a bad thing.

"She's not supposed to," Martin laughed. He had plenty of girls at school offering more than he accepted. She was wifey material as far as he was concerned. He could feel her eyes on his back from above as he continued on. She giggled and ducked out of sight when he turned to confirm.

An hour and a half later they had reached the downtown gym where he trained. Martin gave his cronies a few dollars to keep them busy for the few hours he would be inside.

"Take it easy today!" Martin's instructor warned when he emerged from the locker room. The teen had hurt a sparring partner really bad last week and he didn't want a repeat.

"I will Tony. Promise!" he said and crossed his heart like he had seen people do. He still wasn't sure how that happened since he didn't fully understand his own strength. What he did know was that mortal men felt like toddlers to him when he trained. He recalled the snapping of cartilage when he executed the new submission hold he was taught.

"Good, cuz I'm with you today. Can't get any of these tough guys to spar with you!" Tony said loud enough for the tough guys to hear. Even though they turned heads or looked away, pretending not to hear.

Martin was a natural and picked up each martial art science as easily as he took to science in the lab. The lab was next since his mother had arranged private tutoring with a prominent NYU science professor to round out his day.

Tony intended to teach Martin a new hold designed to make an opponent tap out in two seconds. He quickly found out that Martin had mastered it and two seconds was one second too long. Martin quickly reversed the technique and twisted his arm around his own head.

"Shit Martin!" Tony fussed as he tapped. He and everyone watching knew the kid should be teaching the class, not in it. "How'd you..."

"YouTube," Martin said apologetically as he let him up. It was true since he spent hours studying his craft. Most did but few mastered them just by watching. Not to mention, none possessed the brute strength he had.

"Yeah well, hit the speed bag and uh, yeah..." Tony said over his shoulder and rushed into his office to make sure his arm wasn't broken. The speed bag didn't fare much better as Martin pushed himself to a limit he didn't know he had. All eyes were on him but none could keep up with the blur of his hands.

"Is this shit real?" another student reeled as his hands moved a hundred miles an hour.

"Nah, a trick..." another was saying before the bag tapped out. It literally exploded, sending sand and leather flying like shrapnel.

"My bad!" Martin called out. He rounded out his work out in the weight room pretending that the two hundred pound plates were heavy. He grunted and groaned for show even though he could juggle the weights like tennis balls if he wanted.

"We're gonna be filled up next week. So um, un-huh," Tony stammered when the class came to a close. Martin nodded along with him since he knew he violated one of the

48 laws of power. Not only had he outshined his master but did so publicly. Tony could either turn the class over to him or expel him. He chose the latter since it was his livelihood and all.

He simply went to the studio across the street for his next lessons. Today was sword fighting with a samurai warrior flown in just to train Martin. He was being prepared for a war but didn't know it just yet. When the war came he would be ready.

"What did you learn?" Q asked eagerly when Martin emerged from the gym. There wasn't a trace of disappointments on his face from getting kicked out of class. Instead a relieved smirk twisted the corner of his thick lips.

"That men are bitches," he replied and laughed at the confused looks on their faces. "Let's get something to eat!"

"Hell yeah!" both men cheered. They realized they got far more out of being his friend than his enemy. They were already downtown so they headed over to do iconic Forty Second street to eat with the tourists.

"Let's try this spot?" Martin suggested when they reached a trendy spot. He was paying so he didn't have to wait for an answer.

He didn't intend to wait in the long line either so he approached the front thinking he wished could skip the line. It had worked before and worked again now. The hostess popped her head up and looked directly at Martin.

"Next!" the woman said, extending the table pass needed.

"Hey!" the large white man who was about to get skipped protested on behalf of his party. The group of cops had flown in from Mississippi where niggers came last. "These niggers can't skip us!"

"These niggas will flip you!" Q proclaimed and stepped forward to do just that. Even though he would have been shot down. The cops were out of their jurisdiction but still brought some guns along in the car.

"Chill," Martin said and he chilled. He smirked at the cops and accepted the table pass. The men were still grumbling as they entered the spot and took their table. It could have been over since the next party came in a few minutes later.

"Them niggas want smoke!" Ant-man growled when the table of cops glared over at them. These uppity niggers up north burned their butts.

"I smoke," Martin said as the N-word floated around their table like a rap song. He'd rather eat and head back uptown but was with the shit too. It would be whatever they wanted it to be.

"At home we would have hung them niggers!" the main one said directly at Martin. He wanted smoke and now he was going to get some. Martin smiled and accepted the challenge.

"Not here," he told his crew when they began to stand. They followed his eyes to the various cameras around the room. The last thing he wanted was to get in trouble with Melcina.

Dusk had given way to darkness as both parties wrapped up their dinners, then desert. It was obvious that each was waiting on the other so they all stood at once and headed towards the door.

"No cameras or cops near the water..." Martin said over the noise of the city and headed in that direction. The tourist could keep their plans to see a movie or follow him and be in one. They chose to follow and star in their own movie. They had no idea it was going to be a horror show.

"I'll run to the car..." one of the cops said and did just that as the others followed behind spewing N-words like smoke from a locomotive.

"Six on three," Q said with a timbre of shook in his voice. He had always been a bully and preferred the odds in his favor.

"Mmhm," Martin laughed, since he knew it wasn't enough. A glance back only produced five which meant one punked out early.

The cops joined the black kids near the waterfront and put up their dukes. They all knew why they were here just like a one night stand after the club. No need for small talk since you came to fuck. Q and Ant-man felt the need to protect Prince deep down in their souls so they jumped in front and led the attack.

The big mouth stepped around the fray and confronted Martin. He saw the peach fuzz of facial hair and knew he was a kid. Bad cops love nothing more than beating on black kids. Black men fight back so they prefer kids and women. He saw the sarcastic smile form on Martin's face and took a big swing to knock it off.

"What the..." the cop said when the punch hit nothing but air. It was on perfect track to connect with his chin, but suddenly he wasn't there anymore.

"I know right," Martin laughed as he appeared beside him. Then popped him right in the puzzled look on his face.

"Why you uppity nigger!" the man grunted and swung with everything he had plus a little more since he especially hated uppity niggers even more than regular niggers.

Each swing came up empty along with a pop from a different direction. Q and Ant-man were still trading blows evenly with the other four when the six arrived back from the car. Martin's men were ready to talk shit when the cops suddenly stepped back. Until they saw the reason why pointed at them.

"Prince, he got a gun!" Ant-man screamed to alert their leader. The angels would record them as his last words because two shots slammed into his chest and knocked his life out the two holes in his back.

Martin rushed forward but wasn't yet faster than the speeding bullets that cut Q down next. The gunman turned the gun at Martin and fired again. He had a clear shot but Martin wasn't there when the slugs arrived. He followed with the barrel, squeezing off rounds.

"Oh shit! Shit! Shit!" he fussed when he saw his comrades writhing on the cold concrete from the rounds. Martin had moved in front of the other cops and let them take the bullets for him.

"The fuck are you doing Cletus!" Jimbo screamed. "Shoot the nigger!"

"I'm trying..." he said, chasing the speeding teen with the gun. He fired off the last two rounds and gunned his friend down. The gun clicked empty but he had a bigger problem on his hand as Martin approached. There was nothing else to do except throw the gun at him like in the movies.

"Really?" Martin laughed as he slapped the gun back at him. The man tried to run but Martin ran faster and ended up in front of him. "My turn..."

The redneck, hillbilly, racist cop sounded like he was ready for the Grand Ole Opry when he hit those high notes. And who could blame him since Martin literally broke him into pieces. He snapped both tibias, then fibula. Next went the femurs before moving up to the arm. He sounded like a wounded Dolly Parton when his radius bones broke. Followed by the humerus which Martin found humorous.

"Sing that funky music white boy..." he laughed and cracked his rib cage. Luckily for the redneck Martin was educated enough in anatomy to keep him alive. Maybe lucky, because he was fucked up. He had final instructions before leaving him. "Who did this?"

"I did. I killed my friends, and those niggers," he relayed as Martin suggested into his psyche.

"Gonna have to write it though," Martin said and gave him one last kick that broke his jaws in five places.

CHAPTER 6

"Huh?" Martin asked when he felt the strange, yet familiar sensation.

A feeling he hadn't felt since his parents were alive. At least not this strongly since vampires were increasing in numbers since his mother and father weren't around to kill them. This was just the first time a vampire had been in the same house since Kristine gave Melcina the cure.

"What's wrong with you?" Melcina asked when she finally emerged from her room. "You look like you saw a ghost."

"I um," he began, then paused. Melcina had been a vampire before so it just rang familiar. "You OK?"

"Me?" she asked instead of admitting that she was most definitely not OK. She had a blood thirst that made her feel like a heroin junkie on the verge of withdrawals. "Mmhm, I'm good. Great!"

"Oh, OK. Well I'm getting ready to..." he began.

"Have fun! Need money!" Melcina cut in. She was eager to get him out of the apartment so she could go feed.

"Bed, school tomorrow," he replied and sighed.

"Oh, OK. Yeah. Well, here. Take some money anyway," she said and thrust some bills at him. He was still wondering what was up with her when her bedroom door closed. He shrugged his shoulders and put the money in his pocket. He had finally bagged Ximena's phone number and planned to talk to her until the break of dawn.

Martin was under the steaming water but still heard Melcina's window open since it was squeaky. It wasn't unusual since she often opened it at night to let the cool breeze off the Hudson river flow in. On particularly warm nights they might even camp out on the terrace that ran the length of the apartment.

What was unusual was her easing out the window. Not as unusual as climbing down the array of terraces like a lizard. It was good they lived on the rear of the building so no one on busy Ogden avenue saw the strange sight.

Melcina could hear the beating hearts in the apartments she passed and fought the urge to barge in and dine. This was too close to home since she needed to keep her secret from Martin. Melcina had called ahead and her dinner was waiting when she reached the ground.

"Over here!" Mark called in between beeps on his horn and waved. He was delighted when the pretty young thing called him. His wife had the same old vagina and he wanted something strange. He just had no idea just how strange this chick was.

"Mmmm," she hummed and rushed over into the passenger seat. "Let's go! Somewhere private!"

"Say no more!" he gushed and pulled a reckless u-turn that nearly delayed her feeding. An accident would have meant cops and tickets and statements and she didn't have time for all that.

"Asshole!" a driver shouted and shot a bird as he served

out of the near collision. The hot head driver pulled a u-turn of his own to follow.

"Chill!" Melcina fussed and moved his hand when he reached for her crotch. She had a second thought since she knew what was in his near future and pulled his hand back over. "Here you go."

"Gonna get it nice and wet, like last time!" Mark vowed and worked his fingers. Her box responded but not quite like last time since most of that was deposited by the vampire in the club.

"Mmhm," Melcina said to whatever he said since she wasn't paying attention. She was looking for a secluded spot to feed. "Right there!"

"Here?" he asked but whipped to a stop before she could answer. Melcina took a deep breath and let her fangs extend.

Marks eyes went wide in stark terror but he was looking out the window behind her. People usually had that reaction to her so she turned to see what he was seeing. Turned just in time to see the gun spark. The disgruntled driver from the block fired into the car.

"No!" Melcina screamed as her dinner slumped over beside her. The spray of blood nearly got into her open mouth and that could have been devastating. Only blood from a living, beating heart gives life to vampires. Dead blood can turn them into zombies.

"Watch where the fuck you drive next time!" the man told the dead man and turned to get back into his car. He turned again and raised the gun when he heard the car door open behind him. It lowered when he saw the woman and women are no threat.

"That was my dinner!" she growled and inched forward. Bullets couldn't kill but no one wants to get shot.

"Oh! Are you working? Shoot take the bread out the nigga

pocket!" he shrugged. A split second later he registered her good looks and had another thought. "Shit, I got a few bucks to spend..."

"You'll have to be my dinner then..." Melcina growled. The shooter's head tilted curiously when he saw the fangs. The perfect position to get bitten.

An eerie howl lit up the night as she attacked. Melcina opened wide and snatched his entire throat away. A warm gush of blood hit her face and almost did what Mark's fingers almost did. She grabbed him to hold him up and clamped on the gaping wound. She did come now when the hot blood squirted down her throat. She held on as the flow of blood began to subside. His heart pumped it's last and quenched her animal thirst.

"Now..." Melcina said and twisted her lips. Now she had to figure out what to do with this mess. An idea spread a smile on her face and she dragged him under his car. Her vampire strength allowed her to pull him under the wheel with the tire on his wound. It was the best she could with short notice and skipped happily back home.

"That's what I'm talking about!" Martin cheered when the bacon in his dreams became the bacon of his breakfast. Melcina was back to her old self and that meant breakfast.

"Hey there!" Melcina sang as Martin barrelled into the kitchen. She was humming happily while fixing a big breakfast.

"Um, hey?" he greeted back. His whole being tingled from her presence. Something was different but he vividly recalled this same feeling from his earlier life. From Melcina and his own parents. It was even stronger now after feeding.

"I'm sorry about your friends!" she purred. The news of Ant-man and Q were top stories around the country since the vacationing cop took the rap. The local cops had no explanation for how he got nearly every bone in his body broken.

"Yeah," Martin said and twisted his lips in thought. It would be his first time going to school without his body-guards but he now knew he didn't need them. He wasn't sure what he was, but vulnerable wasn't whatever it was. "You're not eating?"

"Who? No. Big meal last night. I'm on a new diet," she smiled and cast a glance at the window. The sun had just risen, so it would be a while until it set again. A while before she could feed again.

Melcina had no use for human food anymore so she watched the teen scarf his down. She knew what he was even if he didn't. He was an anomaly who didn't need blood to survive and could walk freely in direct sunlight.

"What?" he asked with a mouthful of human food when he saw her watching.

"Nothing. Want me to ride with you to school?" she offered, but only because she knew the answer. This was a rough neighborhood but not as rough as the DNA that made up his body.

"You gonna push me in a stroller?" he shot back. Then laughed to take some of the sting out of the sharp reply.

"I'm going to bed then," Melcina sighed and stood. She planted a kiss on his cheek and headed down the hall. "Have a good day."

Martin nodded that he would since he had a science test this morning. Most of his classmates had studied all weekend but it was all rudimentary to him. The science lessons his mother left were far more challenging. Precisely why he was far more advanced than anyone in his class, including the teacher.

"OK then!" Martin nodded as he admired himself in the full length mirror. Despite the money to buy designer clothes he opted for the trendy clothes of his age group. His muscular frame just made those mundane threads look a little better on him.

"Sup yo. Sorry about your man's ndem," Chico said and dapped Martin up when he stepped from the building. They were cool even though he had kept his distance when Antman and Q were around. They were in the ground now so he pulled up.

"Yeah," he replied, since anything more could be too much. They fell into the back of the line of kids waiting to catch the bus down the hill to Yankee Stadium. From there they would split up on different buses and trains to go to different schools around the city. Ximena boarded a couple blocks later with her friends. The two exchanged smiles and googly eyes for the rest of the way down the hill. They had spoken all night long so the smiles were genuine.

"She not fucking..." Chico said and shook his head as if in mourning. The resurgence of morals and modesty should be applauded, not mourned.

"Good," Martin said through his smile. Her chastity was just as attractive as the pretty face and round ass. They exchanged parting smiles and went their separate ways. They would continue talking all night and smiling all day for the next couple of years.

CHAPTER 7

"Happy birthday to you..." Melcina sang when Martin emerged from his bedroom on his eighteenth birthday.

"Thanks!" he quickly cut in since Melcina did a lot of things well but singing wasn't one of them. They both laughed at the implied joke and shared a hug.

Martin felt the cold clamminess of her between species, but was now used to it. His preoccupation with his own growing up made him ignore the obvious signs of her nocturnal adventures. She was careful about leaving other catastrophic injuries on her victims so she didn't draw heat. Plus she rarely dined locally.

That meant spreading her carnage throughout the five boroughs, and occasionally taking a night off. Two nights would be too many and have her fiending like a dope fiend. Who just happened to be her least favorite meal. They were easy to catch like a sheep but had a bitter aftertaste like a diet soda.

"Another video today!" she cheered happily on the

outside, while internally searching for an excuse to beg off. For two years she had successfully dodged the sunlight by a myriad of excuses. They were aided by Martin's being busy doing his own thing. "Ooh, these cramps!"

"I got it. I'll just relay what they said," he happily replied since Mr Walsh had emailed him to come alone. The yearly videos had always been directed to them both, but this one was for his eyes only. It just confirmed what he was feeling anyway. The child was now a man.

"Great! I better get some rest!" Melcina said and faked a yawn. She did have a busy night since she had to travel all the way to Westchester last night in search of a meal.

She caused a nasty one car accident on the expressway that resulted in a woman nearly being decapitated when she came through the windshield. Melcina sucked the fresh blood through the gaping wound and ran back to the city before dawn.

"You ready?" Martin asked when Ximena took his call as he headed out the apartment.

"Yes!" she laughed and he knew she wasn't.

"Well I'm coming down the block now. So..." he warned. He usually didn't mind the extra time she took to get extra pretty for him, but today he was on someone else's time. Not only did he have an appointment with Mr Walsh, but would get to see his parents again.

"I'm coming papi!" she pleaded, knowing the 'papi' would get him.

"Mmhm," he said and scheduled an Uber since the time to make it by train had just passed.

Martin posted up on her front stoop to wait but didn't have to wait long. Out came Ximena in a flowing sundress that had the opposite effect than what she was going for. She preferred loose dresses and pants to downplay her curves but curves like that really can't be downplayed. A burlap sack would look good on the young woman.

"Sheesh!" Martin gushed at his girl all gussied up. They had made it official a year ago but her virginity was still intact. His vision was sharper than most humans since he was less human than most humans. He saw through the material as it was sheer. Her hard abs were in the middle of two plump breasts straining a cotton bra, and the plump mound of new pussy in the cotton panties. And while most pussy is good pussy, new pussy is the best pussy.

"Stop!" Ximena giggled and blushed at his gawking. Even though he was the only one of the many men who gawked and got a giggle. The rest got a dose of hot Latina temper in a bilingual barrage of curse words.

"You stop!" he laughed just as their ride came. He shook his head at all that ass shaking when he helped her into the car first. The driver greeted cordially and headed downtown.

"I'll be an hour," Martin advised when they reached the lobby of the law firm.

"You told me, twice!" she reminded and retrieved a school book from her bag. "Gives me time to study."

He nodded and turned to the receptionist who ushered him inside. They walked to the room where he usually viewed the videos with Melcina. Her being absent wasn't the only thing that was different. His super sharp sense of smell instantly identified the caustic scent of acid.

"Well hello there Mr Jones!" Mr Walsh greeted and extended his hand. He followed Martin's eyes over the small vat as they shook and went on to explain. "This video is for your eyes only. Once you watch, please insert into the slot.

"OK," he agreed as his curiosity piqued. He almost wanted to turn on the part of his brain that could read thought when he accepted the sealed video. None of the others had been opened, but the sincerity in the man's eyes told the rest of the story. "Thanks."

Martin waited a few seconds after the door closed behind him. He glanced around to see if anyone could see before tearing into the package. The old school DVD read 'Happy 18th' in his mother's unmistakable handwriting.

"Thanks ma," he said and slid the disc into the player. A smile spread across his face when he saw his parents smiling back at him.

'Hello handsome!' his father laughed. Martin got the joke since even he could see they were nearly identical. Not quite twins since his mother had left her mark on his features as well.

'So vain!' his mother laughed and lovingly spanked his hand. Both their faces changed a moment later. Along with Martin to match their somber looks.

'There's no easy way to tell you this son. By now I know you've noticed you're,' Kristine said and paused in search of the right word. 'different.'

'Different?' Martin Sr laughed. 'Son, climb over the railing on the terrace and jump.'

'Don't tell him that!' his mother fussed like a mother. Martin was amused as they went back and forth at how to tell him what they needed to tell him. It was a delightful throw back to watching their intellectual debates at the dinner table. As usual his mother won, which means his father won. She gathered her thoughts and began.

'You're a vampire. A hybrid that makes you smarter, and more powerful than any other vampire,' she said before dad tossed in his two cents.

'And more dangerous!' Martin Sr said, then sat back like he hadn't said anything.

'And you'll need it! Vampires are an abomination. An affront to God. He only created mankind to worship Him, but these creatures are from the devil. It had been my life's work to destroy them...

'Until she married one. Me!' Martin Sr bragged and got a smile from his mother before she continued.

'I have the cure. It depends on the vampire's will. It will kill them or cure them. Your father and I had begun eradicating all vampires from the face of the planet. Werewolves and lycans as well. This world belongs to mankind. These threats will wipe out mankind if we,' she paused, cleared her throat and went on. 'If you don't destroy them.'

'Destroy them all son. We killed as many as we could but I know their numbers are slowly climbing. There is a house on Long Island. There are weapons, instructional videos...'

'And a lab. My formula is there. Reproduce and mass produce. The fate of the world is in your hands,' Kristine said wearily.

"What about me? Will I drink blood? Will I kill people?" Martin yelled at the screen. His parents couldn't hear him but still answered.

'You are good. There is no evil in you. Once you finish your task, take the cure yourself. Live a natural life,' his mother said but that was as far as she could go so his father chimed in.

'And die a natural death,' he concluded, then continued. 'There are no good vampires. Kill them all!'

"Hey ba..." Ximena began but the cheer died in her throat when she registered the distress on his face. The one hour turned into two and a half since Martin had to watch it more than once. "Are you OK baby?"

"No," he sighed and regretted his honesty since he couldn't share it. The weight of the world had just been dropped in his lap. An eighteen year old tasked with the survival of mankind. He wanted to go back and watch the video again but recalled the violent sizzles when he inserted it into the acid. He could only imagine what next year's video would hold.

"Are you hungry?" she asked since she had seen her mother change her father's mood like that. She changed it behind the locked door as well but Ximena wasn't doing that until he was her husband.

"No," Martin said even though his head nodded up and down and his stomach growled loudly as if it heard the question.

"Aww my poor papi!" she moaned with her bottom lip poked out and moved in for a hug. The big breast pressed against him certainly helped a little. His life had changed so dramatically, so quickly, he knew he couldn't sort it out right here in the law firm's lobby.

"Let's get something to eat!" he cheered and extended his elbow. Being smarter than the teachers all through school allowed him to hone his ability to be in two places at the same time. He nodded and smiled along with her banter over lunch, but his mind was a million miles away.

The life changing news came with a healthy deposit in his bank account for a new car. True to his parents instructions he got his license at sixteen but had to continue his driving lessons for two more years before being allowed to buy his first car. Not only had his skill matured in that time but his mind as well.

"Nah..." Martin said and shook his head at the idea to call Melcina before heading over to the car lot. He was eighteen now so he would make his own decision. Not to mention he had to save the world, so he should be able to pick out a car.

"Ju are so odd!" Ximena laughed at his talking to himself. His oddness was mainly due to his not acting like everyone else.

"And ju love it!" he reminded and joined her back in the present and presence. Later would have to wait until later so he would enjoy now. "What's your favorite color?"

"Amarilla!" she cheered and he shook his head. "You asked!"

"I did, but I'm not driving a yellow car!" he vowed. It was a good thing he didn't bet since he ended up purchasing a brand new, yellow Camaro. He initiated the sale but would have to come back in a few days once funds were transferred.

Later was rushing forward as they rode an Uber back uptown. The sights of the city stole their thoughts as they rode. Still Martin had a lot more on his mind as they rode. He felt that same tingle in varying degrees as they rode. There were vampires in Manhattan; he just didn't know what he was feeling. He would one day have to kill them, but first had to learn how.

"What did you say?" Martin reeled as they rode up the hill. He thought he heard what she said but it made no sense coming from her. The driver heard it clearly and nearly swerved into a car.

"I asked if you wanted some head before we reached my building," she repeated as they pulled to a stop in front of her building and expired the invite. Ximena laughed at the look on his face and shook her head. "You've been ignoring me since a hundred and tenth street, but you heard that!"

"Driver, take us back to a hundred and tenth street!" Martin demanded and laughed since he knew the offer was a joke. Some of the virgins in school gave head as a consolation prize but Ximena wasn't like them and he appreciated her for it.

"Love you papi!" she said through her giggles and popped a kiss on his cheek before hopping out and running into her building.

"Love you too," he said to her jiggling butt as she rushed off.

"I've been around a lot of hoes in my day!" the driver offered as they pulled off. He was closer to getting punched in his mouth as anyone can without getting punched. His next words saved him some skin, "And that ain't one! Good women are rare, hold on to her!"

"Gotcha!" Martin agreed and slid a tip forward. It had been a busy day but night would prove to be even busier.

CHAPTER 8

Being eighteen meant not having to ask permission to go out. It was also so close to seventeen Martin figured he'd better ask. His instilled honesty made a lie hard to come by. Even though the truth would be less believable than anything he could make up.

Martin's parents made him vow to keep his secrets to himself. He wasn't even allowed to share it with the woman who was raising him. That's why he had to go to the attorney's office alone. He was still mulling over words that were both true, yet deceptive at the same time.

"Martin, I'm headed out for a while. Hot date!" Melcina cheered happily. She usually went out the window once he went to sleep but was dressed to the nines tonight. The smile on her face was at being able to kill two birds with one fang. Both fangs actually but she was going to get laid first.

"Have fun!" he cheered in relief. A second relief for the day since she didn't ask about the attorney visit. He called Ximena like he would always do, but also to stall.

"Oh, I will!" Melcina laughed mischievously on her way

out. Some dumb dude named Tricky Ricky had camped out in her DM for the last few days. She respectfully declined his advances so he disrespectfully dropped a dick pic. It just so happened to be a nice dick so she would take a ride on it before draining all the blood that made it nice and hard like the picture.

Tricky Ricky was parked right up front when Melcina stepped out of the building. She instantly spotted the car since he had more pictures of it than his kids on his wall. He honked and waved since he had no idea how sharp her sight and hearing was. Nearly as sharp as the fangs she intended to drop into his life just like the dick he dropped into her inbox.

"Well hey there!" Melcina cheered when she slid into the passenger seat. He couldn't even pronounce the word gentleman so no way was he going to open a door. What he didn't know was that gentlemen get rewarded with free crotch shots if the woman is wearing a dress. Especially a tiny one like Melcina was wearing.

"Hey yourself!" he smiled to show off the gold teeth he displayed daily on his social media. He lived across the bridge in New Jersey so he headed up to the hundred and seventy fourth street bridge. The George Washington was a few blocks away and over to Jersey. Just enough time to tell her all the things he was going to do to her when he got her home.

"Nice!" Melcina cheered and soaked his seat since she wasn't wearing panties. No sense putting them on to take them right back off, she reasoned. Plus she was going to drink all his blood anyway so the seats were the least of his worries. They pulled up to the same house he posted on his page so she said, "Nice!"

"Thank you!" he said and hopped out. Melcina just shook

her head and decided not to give him any head for leaving her behind.

"No, I'll get my own door," she said sarcastically as she got out and followed him inside. He led her to the sofa and knelt before her like a delegation to a queen.

"As advertised..." he said and leaned in for a lick. Vampire pussy is actually very sweet, so it's like a going away treat.

"You go boy!" Melcina cheered as he twirled his tongue around her lady parts. He kept his promise to eat her like a fat kid does cake. So much so she actually clapped for him while he ate. "Yay!"

"Mmhm!" Tricky Ricky hummed and nodded since his tongue was too deep inside her for words. He gave himself a mental pat on the back when she began to shiver and quiver from an orgasm. This was a good time to give her the dick so he reached down and rolled a condom on to rush inside of her.

"Hold up!" she protested and held him from entering her. "At least 'lemme see it, touch it. Shoot I may want to return the favor!"

"Huh?" he asked and Melcina twisted her lips into a 'yeah right'. Everyone knows if you can huh you can hear. He knew it too and reluctantly agreed. "Oh alright!"

"That's not the same dick!" she immediately identified. Still she pulled her phone to double check and sure enough, the dick in front of her was half the dick in her DM. "Bruh, did you catfish the dick?"

"Yes," he hung his head and admitted. "Chicks be saying they need more dick so..."

"So, whose dick is it?" she wondered and looked around just in case he was present. He may as well finish off what he started.

"Got it offline," he said and twisted his lips ruefully.

"Awe, I'm sorry," Melcina mourned. She felt bad for him and pulled him inside of her. Tricky Ricky was one of those 'ain't the size of the boat, but the motion in the ocean' dudes and set out to prove it. Taking Melcina by total surprise. "Oh! OK, then..."

"Mmhm," Ricky bragged as he banged on the box like a bongo. It was a game of angles and friction and his guest was soon shivering and quivering once more.

"Well look at you!" she cheered like a kindergarten teacher about to hand out gold stars for the day. She wasn't though so her fangs slid out instead. She did spare him from the horror of seeing them just like he tried to do with the dick.

"Oh?!" he wondered when she pulled him into an embrace he couldn't get out of. Her super sharp fangs slid in so easily the pain was delayed. "Owe! Hey! Help!"

"Mmhm," she hummed and gulped down his life blood. She loosed her grip when he stopped squirming and struggling. Once he was dry she laid him down on the sofa and took his car keys. "I'm going to borrow your car if you don't mind?"

He didn't.

"Just jump..." Martin repeated his father's words as he looked down off the terrace. He had dropped plenty of items over the edge over the years and they all went splat when they reached the ground. The thought shook his head and reminded him of his mother's suggestion.

'Slowly explore your strengths. Take your time, gradually...' Kristine advised.

"I tried that mom," he told her memory and remembered

stacking more and more weight on the bench press at school. Luckily no one saw him manhandle five hundred pounds. It scared him enough to rush from the weight room and never return.

Not that he needed to because he knew he was strong. He wasn't sure how strong but could feel it coursing through his being. He constantly downplayed his strength among mortals. Just because it had been years since he tuned out people's thoughts didn't mean he couldn't hear people's thoughts.

"Just jump?" he asked his father once more. Then jumped, and instantly regretted it. "Oh shiiiiiiiiiit!"

Young Martin saw his young life flash before his eyes as he sped to the ground below. He remembered his mother's practical advice to go slow but it couldn't help him now at a hundred miles an hour. He also remembered how his father used to throw him high in the air but never let him fall. He wouldn't let him fall now.

"Stop!" he ordered inches from disaster. His body stopped it's free fall in an instant. He softly stepped down to the ground. "Fuck!"

Fuck was right when he took a jump to the tenth floor. Then bounded back up to his own terrace. The night was young so he hopped a few flights at a time until he reached the rooftop. He had looked down from the ledge many times over the years and was never afraid of falling.

"Just jump..." he repeated and jumped from twenty six stories above the earth. Once again he stopped a millisecond before the splat. Martin would spend the rest of the night exploring his limits. He could actually fly but didn't know it yet.

Gunshots from the nearby projects caught his attention. This was the Bronx so it wasn't unusual, but the woman's screams that followed beckoned him to investigate. Martin was a blur as he crossed over to the projects, yet could see everything clearly. Including two men firing at two other men firing back.

Kids would usually be tucked away in bed at this time of night but again, this was the Bronx so they were hanging out. Hanging out right in the middle of a gunfight. A woman was screaming louder than her wounded toddler who had taken a round to his chubby thigh.

Two of the men dipped into their building while the intruders jumped into a car to make a getaway. Martin made a quick decision and followed the car as it sped away. He quickly caught up as it pulled out the projects.

"The fuck yo?" the passenger reeled when he saw a person running along side of the barreling car. He checked the speedometer and confirmed, "What the fuck!"

"Clap at that nigga!" the driver shouted and mashed the gas. The passenger leaned out and opened fire. Now Martin got a real glimpse of the speed he possessed. He sped up so much the bullets slowed down. He actually stepped aside and raced one of the rounds before turning back to the car.

"Son! This nigga dipping the bullets B! Dead ass!" the passenger exclaimed. His partner opened his mouth to doubt him but Martin gave the car a nudge with his shoulder that flipped it on it's side. Sparks lit up the dark block as the car slid into a row of parked cars.

That was enough action for one night so he turned and headed back to his building. He cut through the playground to the back. Two bounds later he was back on his own terrace. The safest place he knew was under his blanket so that's where he headed.

He heard Melcina arrive an hour later but didn't budge.

CHAPTER 9

"Come down and check out the new car!" Martin called to the back when he got the call from the dealership.

"Maybe later," Melcina said, meaning nightfall. She held up her book as if it were the reason she couldn't go outside. It was a good book and all but she really just didn't want to burn to ash under the sunlight. Now that she was a vampire she needed to kill a few vampires to get stronger.

"OK!" Martin shrugged since he was still naive enough to ignore the obvious. He was still too green to know the tell-tale signs of a vampire. High school had ended so now it was time for his real lessons to begin. Vampire killing 101, from the world's top vampire killer. His mother.

Martin was glad Ximena had to work her weekend job so he didn't have to make any excuses. Both had been accepted to good universities but no one could teach him what he needed to know except his mother and father. There would be no interns, or CEO training.

"Sup," the Uber driver greeted as Martin slid in the back

seat. Martin usually liked to ride the train for the sights and action but was on a mission today.

"Last Uber for me. Going to pick up my first car!" Martin announced. He had been telling everyone he saw about the car whether they liked it or not.

"That's so cool!" the man cheered and reminisced on his first, many moons ago. It easily filled the gap between the building and the dealership.

Martin signed for his car and hit the road. He entered the address into the GPS system and followed the directions out of the city. Manhattan turned to Brooklyn, then Queens. From Queens to Nassau county and finally Suffolk.

"Uh, and just why couldn't we live out here?" Martin asked his posthumous parents when he turned onto a tree lined street. He chuckled as he could hear his father answer in his mind. "Cuz the Bronx made you tough!"

"It did too pops!" he told the memory as the GPS announced his arrival. He could only shake his head at the pristine high ranch home. The grass was freshly cut, giving the home a lived in look. The door next door opened as soon as he pulled into the parkway. Before he could get the door open a woman was approaching quickly.

"You must be Martin? Yes, you are! I see your mother's features," she rambled. "I'm Mrs Steinberg. My Stuey has been gone for forty years but I'm still Mrs. I'll always be Mrs, never Miss."

"OK Mrs Steinberg," Martin said and stifled a smile at wanting to call her Miss. She looked like she might fight about that so he let it pass.

"Your mother told me, bless her heart! She was a saint you know! And your father! Oy Vey!" she said and bit her lip like she wanted to do something nasty to his father.

"You were saying, my mom?" Martin reminded.

"Oh yeah, a saint. She said you would be here once you graduated school. Welcome to the neighborhood," she said. Martin was finally able to extract himself from the conversation and go inside.

His parents' presence loomed heavy in the house when he walked in. He had walked around, touching things his parents once touched for an hour before he remembered why he was there. He set out in search of a lab but didn't see one.

Martin checked the key against every lock but none matched. A sly smirk spread on one corner of his mouth when he saw a plug cover on an outlet. A quick double check confirmed this was the only plug with a cover in the entire house. He had a bad habit of inserting keys into sockets when he was young. He never got hurt but blew out the power in the building a few times.

This time when he inserted the key the whole wall began to slide to the side. What was on the other side made his knees buckle. Even nearly twelve years later and the equipment was still state of the art. Better than even the labs in the prestigious Bronx High school of science.

"Oh my!" he swooned and grabbed the doorway to keep from falling. Once he got himself together he ventured inside. No kid in a candy store knows exactly where to start, but luckily his mother's prerecorded guide guided him along the way.

'Welcome to the lab son... ' her voice rang through a speaker. The prerecorded message gave him a tour and introduced the equipment. He knew at that moment college would never see him. His place was here.

Time flies when one is having fun and Martin was having a ball. Kristine was light years ahead of anything he had ever seen or heard about. That's saying a lot for the straight A student with scholarships for science. His phone buzzed futilely on the floor. He heard the sound, it just didn't register.

"Ju must got another bitch over there!" Ximena finally shouted into her phone. It had been ringing before going to voicemail for the last few hours but now straight to voice-mail since it was off. She assumed the worst since she wasn't putting out in a city where most girls her age were. Actually the battery went dead since Martin was busy in the lab.

"On God I'ma beat the chick up! I'm coming right now!" she declared and set out to his apartment. It was just before nightfall and she usually had to be home by then.

"Just where are you going chica?" her mother wondered when she marched through the living room towards the door.

"Martin has some bitch over there!" she insisted and smeared the vaseline on her face.

"Oh, handle your business," the mother said since she too would fight a chick over her man.

Ximena stomped up the block to Martin's building. She used to get catcalls and come-ons anytime she left the building but Martin had whooped enough asses around here to stop it. Now teens and men turned their heads and ignored her when she came by.

'Ju may have to give it up,' the devil suggested in her ear as she walked. He hated chastity and morals in people and encouraged sin. 'ju say ju gonna marry him so ju may as well fuck. Try it out...'

"I am. I should. I will!" she said and fell victim to the devil.

She recalled her cycle just came on so it wouldn't be tonight anyway. "Tonight I'ma beat this bitch ass!"

"Knocking like the police! Hope it is the police..." Melcina fussed in response to the angry banging on the door. She hoped it was the police so she could drag them inside and drain them dry. She wouldn't even have to go out in search of her prey. It had been a few days between feedings and she was absolutely parched. Plus the police had an air of arrogance that acted like a good marinade. Cops were delicious.

"Where is he!" Ximena demanded as she barged in. Melcina shook her head as the girl stomped down the hall to his room. She got a whiff of fresh blood when she passed that gave a hunger pang all the way down in her soul.

"Haven't seen him. Not answering his phone," Melcina said and swooned from the delectable smell of blood. Not just any blood, but the best kind. It was almost too good to be true so she had to ask, "Are you a virgin?"

"Excuse me?" the young woman gushed and blushed. Her flushed cheeks answered before her head nodded. "We are not having sex! That's why he's with that other girl now!"

"Mmmm," was all Melcina could hum. The thought of some good, fresh virgin blood, untainted by sin and semen made her knees buckle. It was all she could do not to attack the girl on the spot. Only the love Martin had for her spared her. She would not kill his girlfriend.

"I was going to put out, once my period ends. Now, I'm done! I quit him!" Ximena fussed. She pulled her phone and said the same into his voicemail. "It's over! I quit ju!"

"Are you sure?" Melcina asked and cocked her head. Ximena heard the threat in her tone but didn't know how to apply it.

"Its over!" she insisted and spun on her heels. The movement sent another puff of her essence in the air. The flowing blood made Melcina's mouth water. Melcina waited until she heard the elevator door open and close before she moved. Then made her move out the back and over the edge of the terrace.

"Hey cutie! Hey ju!" Ximena flirted as she stomped back down the block. These same dudes used to hound her but no they turned their heads and ignored her. One got up and ran off just in case Martin was coming. "Punks!"

Night had fallen but she wasn't ready to go inside just yet. Go inside and do what when the love of her life was doing some chick. She turned the corner and headed over to Nelson park. Kids played on its offerings during the day, but the freaks came out at night.

Junkies turned tricks with dicks on the benches, swings and even monkey bars. A woman showed both ingenuity and dexterity as she hung upside down from the bars with a man in her mouth. It's a few bucks extra but probably worth it.

"Pssssh!" she huffed at the sex act, assuming her boyfriend was getting some acrobatic head at the moment. A ruffle of wind spun her around to find no one behind her. The swings were unoccupied and made a perfect perch to sit and pout. She kicked her legs to get the swing swinging when another ruffle turned her head. Again she turned to find nothing but found someone when she turned back around. "Shit Melcina! Ju scared me!"

"Yeah..." Melcina agreed and looked around as her fangs slowly slid from her gums. "You should be scared."

Melcina moved quicker than the girl could process. The next thing she knew she was locked in a vice-like grip with a sharp pain in her neck. The vampire moaned as the sweet virginal blood slid down her throat. It was like that first, cold sip of Wild Irish Rose to a dedicated wino. Ximena struggled in protest, making the chains of the swing jingle loudly. Loud enough to be heard by a cop who swung by for a mid shift blow job. He didn't mind paying the few extra dollars for some upside down head.

"Hey!" he fussed and shined his light in the direction of the sounds of struggle. He blinked when the two figures became one figure quicker than he could figure. His mind accepted his eyes, made an error and focused on the one remaining person. "You alright?"

"No!" Melcina shouted back in confusion. She had no idea of what just happened to her. What she did remember was, "My boyfriend is with some bitch!"

"Yeah, well so am I," the cop shrugged and inserted his private part in the public mouth. He clutched the agreed upon twenty bucks until she finished her duties. He would release it to her, the second she released him.

Meanwhile, Ximena wobbled back towards her building. The pain throbbed in her neck but she didn't want to touch it. She didn't recall any of the steps that led her to her front door. Or using the key to get inside.

"Mmhm," her mother hummed in warning as she stumbled through the house. She was too busy watching a singing program on the TV to notice the holes in her daughter's neck. Ximena fell on her bed and died.

"Damn cop!" Melcina fussed at her meal being interrupted. Most virgins around these parts were too young to go missing without a fuss. She was still stomping and pouting when she reached the iconic stairs on one hundred and sixty seventh street. They had been famous long before the Joker did his little dance in the movie.

"Hey ma," a young thug greeted and wiggled his brows flirtatiously. The pit bull he had on a leash whined and pulled away. "Chill Zeus!"

"Yeah Zeus, chill," Melcina cosigned and looked around.

No one was coming up or going down at the moment so she seized the moment by seizing the teen and the dog. It was a tie as to who yelped louder when she dragged them both to the middle of the stairs.

"Chill lady!" were his last words when the lady vampire sank her fangs into his jugular veins.

"Mmmm! Mmhm!" she hummed to both the taste and the struggle. First off he was a virgin himself since he was years younger than he looked and a lot less thug. Then the struggle. They always struggle and it helps increase the heart rate which makes it easier to feed.

"Chill Zeus," Melcina laughed to herself at the whimpering dog. She gave him something to whimper about when she pulled his jaws wide open and placed them over the two neat holes made by her fangs. Then squeezed them closed and tore away his flesh with his canine teeth.

It removed the trace of her fangs but wouldn't explain the loss of blood. Either way, tonight was going to be a problem.

CHAPTER 10

"Shit!" Martin fussed when the strange feeling registered in his stomach. The hunger pang forced him to take a break from the microscopes and specimens.

He was every bit the scientist as his mother and her work fascinated him. It was far more advanced than anything they covered in school. Still he was up to the task since the assignments and clues his mother left in the yearly videos had prepared him for this day. Except this was the next day.

"Shit!" he repeated when he looked at the sun outside the window and realized it was after noon. His parents both taught him to read the signs in creation so he would glance up for the time before glancing down at his watch.

"Shit, shit!" he added for his dead phone. He suddenly remembered he had a hot blooded Latina lady and she was going to let him have it for not spending any phone time with him last night. She would have to wait since his phone was completely dead. He placed it on the charger and headed outside.

"Well hello there Mr Jones! Late sleeper are we?" Mrs Steinberg asked when she popped out of nowhere.

"Huh?" he blurted from the shock, then caught his bearings. He did learn quickly so he told his story walking so she wouldn't hold him up. She was the only one of the two who was retired, he had things to do. "Good morning ma'am. No, I've been up for a while. Going to grab a bite..."

"Try Gold's delicatessen! The Reuben is to die..." she called after the Camaro as it growled down the block.

The Reuben was good but not worth dying for as Martin discovered. No food is, so he scarfed the sandwich down on the way back to the house. As eager as he was to get back to the lab he knew he had to call his girlfriend. His first call went straight to voicemail so his second call went home.

"Hey," Melcina greeted groggily from her long night.

"Hey, I'm..." he began then stopped short. His parents spoke to him alone so he decided against sharing any aspect of their conversation. That included the house on the island. "Has Ximena been by?"

"Uh, yeah. Looking for you. Where are you?" she quickly deflected and made him the subject.

"On my way home. Be there in a few," he sighed since he didn't want to leave. He said his goodbye and headed back out of the house. Heat on his neck turned his head to see Mrs Steinberg peering out a window. It now made sense why his parents chose this house with the nosey neighbor. She would keep a close eye on the property like built-in security.

"Shit," he fussed when Ximena's phone went to voicemail again. It reminded him of the thirty voicemails in his own phone so he checked as he drove. The first twenty were hangups from his hot tempered girlfriend. The last ten were breakups in two languages.

"Shit!" he fussed again and pressed harder on the gas

pedal. So hard the massive engine propelled the yellow car into a yellow blur. Cops like yellow blurs and one fell in behind him. Once he matched Martin's hundred miles per hour he threw his lights on. "Shit!"

All Martin could think about was his angry girlfriend when he pulled over to the shoulder. The cop ran the plates for wants and warrants but found none. The brown skin was still a threat so he rested his hand on his gun when he got out and approached.

"Is there a problem officer?" Martin asked as if he hadn't been just doing a hundred miles an hour.

"You tell me?" the cop asked from behind his dark glasses. They weren't quite dark enough to hide the malice in his eyes. Nor did Martin need to go inside his thoughts to know what he was thinking.

"Besides driving too fast, nothing. Are you going to issue me a ticket?" he answered and asked.

"No need to be hostile! Step out of the vehi..." he began to shout and pull his weapon until he lost control of his own free will.

"There's no problem here. Slow it down and have a nice day," Martin decided for him.

"There's no problem here. Slow it down and have a nice day," the cop repeated whether he liked it or not. He hated it but was powerless to stop it. He found himself back in his car watching the yellow Camaro pull away.

"Oh shit!" Martin reeled at his new found power. It was just the tip of the iceberg of what he could do. He smiled broadly at the immediate benefits. Not only was Ximena going to forgive him, "I'm going to get some pussy!"

"Mmhm!" Ximena's mother hummed when she saw Martin approach from her window perch. She was stationed there most of the day so she could watch the block like the soap opera that it could be. She knew everything going on around there except what was happening in her own house.

"I know. I'm in trouble," Martin smiled up at her. "Tell her I'm here?"

"She hasn't gotten up yet. Cried herself to sleep over ju,"the woman fussed.

"OK. Tell her I'm home. Call me when she gets up," he ordered. The woman's head nodded up and down in agreement despite wanting to say no. Martin had used his ability to make people do what he wanted once again but wasn't done.

"Sup Martin. Sweet whip!" one of the teens from his building cheered when he pulled up to the building.

"Thanks Scrap. Keep an eye on it," he said over his shoulder and locked the kid in place. His plans for the day had flown out the window with the order.

The house was dark with all of the blinds pulled tightly closed. The still unidentified tingle swept through his being when he entered. He was a vampire radar but didn't know it yet. His mother's research fascinated him but also kept him up all night. His body had rights on him so he quickly showered and went to bed. It would be nightfall when he next awoke. He wasn't the only one who awoke with the rise of the moon.

"Hey there!" Melcina greeted happily when Martin emerged from his nap.

"Hey yourself!" he cheered back since she had cooked his favorite fried chicken.

"Figured you would be hungry. I have a date..." she said. Martin noticed she always had an excuse not to eat but was still too naive to read into it. He dug in while she headed out to feed. He felt her presence wane as she headed down the hall. A minute later he felt it return and ring the doorbell.

"Forgot your key?" Martin asked as he pulled the door open.

"Huh?" Ximena asked with a confused look on her face. Not just because she didn't understand the question but, everything seemed strange since she awoke from the dead.

"Never mind," he said and stepped aside so she could enter. He was just glad she wasn't cursing him out. "Hungry?"

"Yes! I'm starving!" she reeled since she understood that. She rushed over to the table since she was hungrier than ever before in her life, or so she thought. It wasn't hunger, it was thirst. She snatched a piece of chicken from his plate, then paused.

"What?" he asked when she stopped short of actually eating.

"I, I, don't know?" she asked, but Martin couldn't help her with that. He could help her with the other feelings coursing through her body. Electric currents that made a vagina throb and form a puddle in her panties.

"Whoa!" Martin laughed when she attacked. The tongue down his throat cut off any other words. Each fondled the other as they had in many make out sessions over the years. This one took a different turn when she pulled away and peeled off her jeans. A few seconds later she was completely naked and fine as the proverbial fuck. "Fuck!"

"Yes please!" she demanded and went for his zipper. She roughly stripped him just as naked and shoved him over to the sofa. The brute strength he felt gave him pause but he forgot it when she climbed on top of him.

Martin watched in wonderment as his virgin girlfriend reached down and gripped his dick. He had deflowered a couple of virgins and knew to go slow and easy. Ximena instead shoved him inside of her and rocked violently. She let out a guttural growl like nothing he had ever heard before.

"Grrr, grrr, grrr," she growled and groaned as she grinded on the dick deep inside of her. At that pace it didn't take long until her fine frame shook and shivered from a violent orgasm.

"Shit!" Martin moaned since he was a second behind her. He was torn between the unprotected sex and the good tight pussy gripping his dick. He decided he would just become a daddy because he didn't have the will power to pull out. Ximena had other ideas when she abruptly stood. "Huh?"

"I have to go!" she blurted and scrambled to get dressed. Martin tilted his head and wondered what the fuck just happened for several moments after the door had closed behind her.

The strange feeling urged Ximena back down the block and into her building. Her mother was still in the window when she returned. The woman had been fussing when she left and picked up right where she left off.

"Ju think ju grown now..." she said down from the window, then waited until she walked into the apartment to finish. "Ju come and go when ju feel?"

"I don't feel...I feel...funny?" Ximena moaned. Her mother came over and placed the back of her hand on her forehead to check for fever. She quickly pulled it away from the cold clamminess of her skin.

"Mmhm! I smell the sex on ju!" the woman reeled back and back handed the girl. The hot box between her own legs got her stuck with a baby at an early age and she wanted more for her daughter. The slap opened a cut in the girl's lip. The taste of blood awakened the animal inside of her. Her mother was still going on as her fangs slid from her gums for the first time. "Ay Dios Mios!"

"Not god, the devil..." Ximena corrected and attacked. She bit her mother's whole throat away and basked in the spray of blood. She had semi quenched both desires with the sex and the blood. The night was young so she set out in search of more.

CHAPTER 11

"It was a particularly bloody night in the Bronx..." a news reporter reported on the morning news.

"And that's news?" Melcina quipped and quickly moved to change the channel.

"Hold up!" Martin said and pulled the remote control away before she could get it. She had no choice but to watch and listen to the grisly reports and hold her breath in case her crimes were featured.

'Fifteen year old Samuel Turner was killed on the stairs leading to one hundred and sixty seventh street in what police are calling a bizarre incident. A source inside the apartment says it may be linked to last night's brutal homicide on Ogden avenue...'

Both Martin and Melcina perked up when they heard their street name. He popped to his feet when his girlfriend's building appeared on the screen. Melcina prepared her excuses since flight nor flight were options. The bright sun was just rising so she couldn't run.

'Carmela Rodriguez was found murdered in her apartment...'

"That's Ximena's mom?" he said to her relief. "She was here last night."

"Ximena, or her mom?" Melcina wondered since she assumed she killed the girl. He frowned at the odd question on his way out the door. He almost forgot he had a car when he ran from the building but the same kid was in the same place keeping the same eye on it.

"Go home Scrap!" he yelled and ran by. It would be quicker to run the two blocks than to drive and park. His Phone was in his hand but Ximena's phone was still ringing when he reached her block.

He looked up to the window hoping to see, so it wouldn't be true. She was tagged and bagged down at the morgue so her perch was vacant. One thing New York city police could do was clear a crime scene. Crimes not so much, but there wasn't a trace of the violence when he ran inside and up to the door.

Yellow police tape crisscrossed the door but didn't slow him from running through all of it. Metal and concrete splashed when he burst inside. He opened his mouth to call out for his girlfriend but the gory scene took his breath away.

This was Ximena's first kill so there was more blood on the floors, walls and ceiling than she got to drink. A seasoned vampire won't let a single drop get by them. Her second kill of the night was somewhat better. A homeless man living in the subway was next to get it. Ximena learned very quickly not to venture out in the sun when she attempted to leave the tunnel. She was still there now, waiting for night to fall.

"The fuck..." Martin wondered and dialed her phone again. He understood why she wasn't answering when he heard it buzzing under the sofa. There was nothing more to see here and too much to figure out on his own. He needed his parents' help so he headed back to his car and back out to the island.

"Let's see..." Martin hummed as he began his search. He had been so caught up in the technical parts of the research he neglected to learn how to track vampires. Luckily his mother left a video labeled, 'how to track vampires'.

'You won't have to see, smell or hear vampires to know them. You'll feel them' his mother explained, then went into detail.

"Oh shit! Shit! Fuck!" he exclaimed along with each detail. When Melcina had turned it didn't fully register since she had been a vampire before in his lifetime. He could only sit and reflect on when she had changed once more. His eyes went wide again when he remembered the same feeling from Ximena. "Shit!"

"Hello there young ma..." Mrs Steinberg called Martin as he ran back out to his car. He blurted his reply and dialed Ximena again. The memory of her phone under the sofa shook his head. He hung up and tried Melcina.

Martin sped back towards the city well above the speed limit. Only because he had yet to explore the limits of his own powers. He could have flown into the city in half the time. He saw the moment a trooper spotted him and glanced down at the speedometer. He didn't have time to deal with getting pulled over so he said so.

"Find something else to do," he suggested and the officer turned his lights back off and backed off.

He had to do it two more times as he made his way back

uptown and found himself back in front of Ximena's building. He looked up in hopes of her mother being right back at her post so this whole episode wouldn't be true. She wasn't though, and things would never be the same.

"Martin? Martin Jones right?" a man asked as Martin stepped out of his car. Martin went inside his head to answer his own questions before speaking. He knew he was a homicide cop, looking for the same person he was looking for. That meant Ximena wasn't here.

"I don't know where she is?" he replied to the next question in the cop's mind. "Not since last night."

"Huh? How," the cop reeled at him answering questions before he could ask them.

"No, I can't come down to the station to answer a few questions," Martin replied and laughed at his confusion. Still he had things to do so he sent him on his way.

"Either come down and give a statement voluntarily, or..." the cop said just like cops say. Martin didn't have time to be wanted for murder so he agreed to follow him down. His own phone along with the building's security cameras would confirm he was home all night. Night had fallen by the time he walked back out of the precinct.

Martin had some questions of his own when he pulled up to the building. He almost expected to see the same kid in the same place when he pulled in. Another group of teens occupied the spot and got deputized to watch the car.

"Can we watch your car?" one asked just like Martin inspired him to do.

"Sure!" he agreed and handed him a twenty dollar bill to go with the mind control. Both elevators had just departed when he walked into the lobby so he hit the stairwell. A few seconds later he emerged on the sixteenth floor.

"Fuck!" Martin exclaimed, amazed by his own speed. It

was still a mere drop in a very big bucket of things he could do.

He knew the apartment was empty since he didn't feel Melcina inside. Still there was plenty left to do so he began a search of her room. At the same time Ximena arrived back at her apartment but she wasn't alone.

"Is that..." the homicide detective wondered when the young woman he was looking for walked right by his car and into the building. She was dirty from a night and day underground and had a confused look on her face.

He got out and pulled his gun since this was a murder case. They didn't find the weapons that caused the massacre which means she could very well still have them on her. She did since he was a weapon.

"So this happened..." Ximena sighed as she entered the crime scene. The tape was gone since the building super planned to clean and rent it out as soon as possible.

"X, uh za, Mina?" the detective asked as he came in behind her. He held his gun at his side so he wouldn't scare her.

"Ximena. It's not hard," she said, looking him up and down. He did the same and noticed the layers of dirt from the underground. She noticed and slid her clothes off while he kept watching. "I need a bath..."

"No, I..." he said but she already turned and headed to the bathroom. Her heavy butt cheeks beckoned so he followed. Not without looking at his watch to see if there was time to fuck her before taking her to jail.

Ximena didn't even register the scalding hot water that rinses the blood and grime down the drain beneath her. The cop registered the erection growing in his pants. He threw caution to the wind and whipped it out. They locked eyes while he gave it a few pulls. Neither registered the danger that approached from the rear until it was in the bathroom.

"What did you do to me?" Ximena asked past the cop. He turned just in time to see Melcina reaching for him.

"Argh!" he gasped when the vampire lifted him off his fluttering feet by his throat.

"Gave you life," she replied and used a claw to open a gash along the man's jugular vein. Ximena moved quickly and caught the first arch of blood before it hit the ceiling.

"Mmmm," she hummed as she closed in and sucked ferociously.

"That's it. Drink up..." Melcina cooed and stroked her long black hair."I gave you life. New life. But, now you have to die."

Ximena lifted her head to process the words but there wouldn't be enough time. Melcina extended her claws and took a swipe that nearly decapitated her. She used her bare hands to finish what she started and snatched her head the rest of the way off.

The still beating heart sent a gusher of blood like a volcano. She was right there to catch it and the powers that came from killing a vampire. A tingle set off alarms as she dropped the empty shell to the blood drenched floor.

"Melcina!" Martin shouted behind her but the shock held him in place.

She let out a high pitched hiss like an angry, feral cat. They were both frozen in fear but it was she who moved first. She burst through the small window in the shower and landed below. She was blocks away before Martin could muster the energy to move.

"What the..." he wondered when he saw the vampire fangs in the detached head. It now made sense when he felt her arrive last night, thinking she was Melcina. Which brought him to, "Melcina is a vampire!"

'There are no good vampires. Kill them all!' his father's words rang in his head.

"Not even Melcina?" he asked aloud but the carnage answered the question for him. He saw the flashing lights of approaching police cars and had to move. His move towards the door was thwarted by tires screeching and radios squawking.

It only took a second to decide that if she could do, so could he. Martin dove arms first like Superman out the window and to his surprise flew, just like Superman.

"Oh shit!" he chuckled as the ground sped by beneath. "I can fly!"

CHAPTER 12

Melcina stayed a few steps ahead since she helped raise the kid into the man he was becoming. His parents were guiding him but she knew how he thought. Like most unscrupulous people she would use it against him. Then again, vampires aren't particularly known for their scruples.

She slinked into a bar on Gun hill road an hour before sunrise. She was full from a few feedings along the way but was now in search of refuge from the rising sun. Going home wasn't an option now that her secret was out.

"Hey now!" An aging pimp named Zach cheered when he spotted the new meat enter the bar.

"Chill grandpa!" A younger pimp laughed and beat him to her. "Sup ma, who you wit?"

"You, if we leave now!" She said as her internal clock ticked loudly.

"Shit, last call ain't for another..." He was saying until there was no one to say it to since Melcina walked off.

"Move too quick, you get seasick!" The older man laughed as she scooped her arm under his.

"Live close?" She asked as they stepped out onto the sidewalk.

"Right around the corner!" He said and escorted her to his pimp mobile. He held the door like a gentleman even though he was a pimp and that's as far from a gentleman as can get.

A few minutes later they arrived at his building with a few minutes to spare. She could feel the heat of the sun just below the horizon.

"What is this place?" Melcina asked as they entered the building. It smelled old with a whiff of death in the air.

"Senior living," he explained. Zach just did a little part time pimping to augment his SSI and Medicaid. It saved some lives too since she didn't dine on the elderly. They tasted sour and gave her the runs.

"Really?" She asked when he popped a little blue pill when they entered.

"Yup. Give me thirty, thirty five minutes and I'ma beat it up real good for you," he vowed.

Thirty five minutes later he kept his word but Melcina missed it since she was sound asleep after a long night.

"Home sweet home," Martin sighed as he pulled up to the house on Long Island. He was smart enough to figure out both that the Bronx was training and that training was over.

He spent the night trying to find Melcina but she stayed a few steps ahead of him. What he did find, or feel was the presence of several other vampires in several other spots throughout the city. He was a vampire killer but first needed to learn how to kill them.

The memory of his decapitated girlfriend was definitely a start. There was plenty left to learn so he hit the lab to learn in all. College was now in session. Last night's revelations gave a sense of urgency since vampires were reproducing.

"How's about a little head?" Zach suggested when they awoke the next afternoon. Most pimps like a test drive before putting a hoe on the road.

"Be careful, I bite..." she warned.

"Eat the dick then!" he dared, dropped his pants and wiggled his old dick and deflated balls.

"Remember, you said to," she said and leaned in. Her fangs slid out as she did and took a bite. mPoor Zach couldn't make sense of what he just saw. Afterall, it's not everyday that a guy gets his dick bitten off.

"Huh?" he asked in search of clarity.. He didn't like the answer though because she spit his dick on the floor and pulled him into a hold he couldn't get out of. He let out a high pitched scream that couldn't be heard by anything but canines.

"Aht-aht," she told herself and refrained from draining him dry. A tiny tourniquet stopped the bleeding but didn't save his life. He died from the bite but would awake again as a vampire.

An opportunist never lets an opportunity get by so she acted the first chance she got. It didn't take Melcina long to realize most of the elderly residents didn't have family or friends. Expendable types, no one would miss. Perfect specimens to turn and kill for more strength. She would need it too because Martin was getting stronger himself.

❄

Martin kept himself busy with the lessons and formulas left behind by his mother. She often left pieces out of the puzzles for him to figure out on his own. Two more years flew by and it was time to move on. There would be no more videos at the attorney's office since he was plugged into the network. He wasn't at all surprised when he saw his parents' faces appear on the screen.

"Happy birthday son!" Kristine cheered broadly as if she could see the handsome man her twenty one year old had grown into. She went on and on while his father waited his turn to speak.

'Your training is now complete. It's time for you to finish what we started. To rid the world of creatures not of it. Vampires, witches, warlocks, werewolves and lycans.' Martin Sr said. As he spoke the accent wall began to slide to the side like a pair of panties to give up the goodness behind it.

"Oh my!" Martin reeled and felt a throb down below. The display of exotic and specialized weapons made his dick hard. Especially the large silver, Excalibur sword hanging dead center. He had been trained by the best in the world to wield this weapon. "I'ma be like Blade out this bitch!"

'Blade ain't got shit on the Dark Prince!' his father said like he heard him. He didn't need to since knew how he thought. Plus this blade did a lot more than the one the movie character carried.

"Oh shit!" Martin said when he ran through a medley of what it could do. A switch lit the blade into a brilliant orange glow that could cut through cold steel like a hot knife does butter.

Then, the guns. Every known submachine gun was present like it was a roll call. There were crossbows with exploding arrows. Electric lassoes, shields and throwing stars. All the things he had trained on his whole life. Just like his parents insisted on two years of driving lessons before getting his own car. His weapons training was complete, it was time to kill.

"No cape?" he chuckled since he had everything else.

'No cape son,' Kristine said and shook his head. "You are no longer Martin Jones. From now on you are the Dark Prince!'

'Wear it well son. We'll see you when you get here,' his father said and the screen went black.

"Guess it's time to kill some vampires!" he said and stood.

"Hmp?" Prince wondered when he arrived at his first destination. His head tilted curiously at the sign on the Bronx assisted living facility, but the now unmistakable presence of vampires was loud and clear.

"Only one way to find out..." he shrugged and got out of his car. Vampires are nocturnal creatures so daytime is the best time to hunt them. Not just because they rest but they can't flee into the sunshine as well.

The smell of death hung heavy in the thick air of the lobby. Blood had been shed here, lots and lots of blood. The elderly residents looked wearily at the newcomer with the sword by his side. They looked old and feeble in wheelchairs and walkers until he was surrounded.

"Soups on!" a woman hissed and tossed her walker aside. She bared her fangs and claws, causing a chain reaction.

"Let's eat then!" Prince grinned and unsheathed his weapon. He decided not to go nuclear and wielded it like a conventional sword. The first swipe took the leader's head clean off. A male vampire approached from the rear but Prince's senses were so sharp it was like he had eyes in the back of his head. He pulled a star and hurled it into his forehead.

It would have been harmless in itself but this one was filled with the vampire killing formula he perfected. The man shook and sizzled as the liquid sunshine spread throughout his body. A red mist filled the air like light rain and body parts fell like hail.

"Queen!" one vampire screamed and took off. The old man pulled the elevator doors open with his bare hands and ran up the shaft like a squirrel does a tree.

"Take me to your leader..." he laughed and followed the scent up the stairs. He chopped off heads and threw the stars as he went along. The presence of vampires steadily decreased as he went up.

"Uh-oh!" Prince thought when he reached the top floor of the building. There was only death below but he felt the presence of at least a hundred vampires behind the door. His shoulders shrugged since his machine pistols both held fifty rounds. Each gel filled bullet contained his patent pending liquid sunshine.

He couldn't help not to smile as he slid his Blade shades on his face. A press of a button on his watch started his father's music playing in the wireless earbuds. They did a lot more than just play music but it was time for some vintage Dark Prince while the son went to work.

A kick to the door sent it flying across the room. It picked up a vampire on the way and sailed out the window. The screams of it sizzling in the sunshine diminished as he fell to the earth. Prince lifted the pistols to spray the crowd but there was no crowd.

"Been waiting on you..." Melcina said down towards him.

She was so tall her neck was bent so she could fit under the ceiling.

"You've been busy I see," Prince said and they both nodded in agreement.

Melcina had indeed been busy over the last few years since people kept dropping unwanted parents off at the facility. She would promptly turn them so she could kill them and grow stronger. The hundred or so vampires he sensed were all inside of her. She left some as security for this day but he made quick work of them.

"So have you," she said of his array of weapons. "You're going to need them."

"Or not..." he dared and dropped the pistols. That would have been too easy and she needed to pay for Ximena.

"What the..." she reeled when he turned into her. An exact replica of Melcina down to the large fangs. That only seemed to infuriate her more and she attacked. Melcina was a black blur as she sped across the room. Her fangs were an inch from taking his face off until he disappeared. She spun to find herself sending a kick in her direction and got kicked in her nose when he appeared on the other side.

"Yeah, I see you learned a trick or two since you've been gone..." she said, morphing into a large lioness.

"Yeah, no, that's not enough!" he said and began to change himself. His parents hadn't taught him this part since some lessons have to be learned by themselves. Her doing it was all he needed to know he could do it as well.

A moment later a forty foot python filled the room. Melcina made a move to bite it's midsection but wasn't fast enough. She quickly found herself wrapped in it's vicelike coils. The sound of all the air escaping her lungs was quickly chased away by the cracking of bones breaking.

"Martin! It's me!" Melcina pleaded as she morphed back into his loving babysitter.

"I know," the talking snake said and kept on constricting. Tighter and tighter, not allowing her to take another breath. It was debilitating but not fatal. She was uncomfortable, but wouldn't die. So he swallowed her whole. The acids in the snake's stomach quickly digested the meal, and shitted her out the other end.

"Next!" Prince laughed when he returned to his original form. His chest filled with pride as he began his life work. There can be only one and he was that one.

CHAPTER 13

Prince had learned many things about vampires from his parents but some things he had learn on his own. The fact that lady vampires have some very, very good pussy was one of those things. His father certainly couldn't share that tidbit via video with his wife right beside him. Vampire killing became that much more fun when he discovered that fun fact.

"Welcome to the Afterlife," a burly bouncer greeted when Prince arrived at the clandestine door. His knowledge of the club's existence was invite enough since it was invite only. Predators invited their prey to party, fuck and die.

"Thanks," Prince replied and tilted his head. The man was mortal which intrigued him. He never understood the alliances between the species. Vampires often keep humans around with the promise of turning them. In turn they did the many things they couldn't do in the daylight.

His eyes automatically adjusted to the dim interior when he walked inside. He inhaled the essence of more humans than vampires and hoped he hadn't struck out again. A few of these places only held pretenders and wannabes. A smirk lifted a corner of his mouth when he spotted her on the dancefloor. The sway in her hips was just as hypnotic as her dark eyes.

The mortal man in front of her was stuck like a fly who flew into a spider's web. He was a healthy specimen who would make a nice meal for a hungry vampire. After she got her rocks off that is. Men used to use her and lose her so now she thrilled them and killed them.

'I gotta go' Prince suggested as he approached the dance floor.

"I gotta go?" the man asked since he was confused by the sudden thought that spilled out of his mouth. She willed for him to stay but he turned and walked off. The competing forces in his head made his nose bleed.

'Hey beautiful,' Prince thought when he felt the woman trying to penetrate his mind. He was too strong so he sent the thoughts telepathically. That and how he would like to fuck her.

"My favorite!" she cheered on the back shots he suggested as he replaced her dance partner. They engaged in a little dirty dancing foreplay before Prince sent her a bright idea. "Let's get out of here!"

"Let's!" he agreed when he read what she had in her mind. She planned to suck him, fuck him, then suck him. She was going to have to settle for two out of three.

"Welp," the bouncer mourned as Prince led the woman by the hand. He longed for the day he could rule the night and feed.

"Soon..." the woman assured him in passing. They made their way out to where Prince was parked. She nodded approvingly at the new Benz since wealthier people usually tasted healthier.

"That would be dope!" Prince said of the wicked thought she thought on her own. She blew him a kiss and dipped down into his lap. It was a short drive to the midtown hotel where he kept a room. Minutes later he was delivering solid back shots in the moonlight flooding in the window.

"My turn!" she shouted after shivering through the first orgasm of the night. She roughly flipped him onto his back and shoved him inside of her. The perfect position to feed once she got off.

Prince did his part by grabbing her hips and thrusting upwards to meet her. They found a rhythm and it wasn't long before she was humming and coming once more.

"Wow, that was good!" she panted and writhed. "I almost hate to do this to you."

"Do what?" he asked as if he didn't know. He did and tilted his head a little as her fangs slid out of her gums. His eyes went wide when she pinned his arms to the side and leaned in for a bite. "Noooo!"

"Hmp?" she wondered when her sharp fangs couldn't penetrate his skin.

"Try the other side," Prince offered and rolled his head to the other side. Why she thought she would be able to penetrate that side is anyone's guess but she quickly found out she couldn't.

"What, what are you?" she asked and let his hands free.

"The one," he replied and pulled her by the back of her head. His fangs had no problem entering her skin. A rush of blood gushed into his mouth but he didn't drink. Instead he pulled the wooden stake from the side of the bed and drove it through her black heart.

"The Meet market huh?" Prince repeated when he found a spot said to be frequented by supernatural types. He had knocked such a dent into the vampire population over the years that the other species began to become more noticeable.

The prototype for the Meet market was down in Mexico city where the laws were lax and missing people were just missed. Most supernatural species understood their survival depended upon their secrecy.

"Not werewolves tho. They obviously don't have a fuck to give!" he fumed at the carnage he seen in pictures. Now it was time for a first hand look.

The millions left behind by his parents allowed him to focus on the work. His life work was ridding the planet of creatures and leaving humanity to humans.

"Psssh!" he hissed at the carnage caused by humans. If not for his parents directives he would have said fuck them and let the best species win. "I gave my word..."

Prince didn't dare love again until his work was done. A steady flow of females of both species kept his appetite satisfied. He prefered vampires since there were no strings attached since he killed them afterwards.

His millions made travel easier with private jets but sometimes he liked to fly coach. Just for the excitement since people are crazy. When he really wanted a dose of real crazy he would take Greyhound. Those people are really fucked up.

"I hope they don't sit us near any of those people," a white lady snarled at the black family ahead of her as they boarded the plane.

"No worry there," her boyfriend sighed and tried not to laugh when that same black family stopped in the first class section while they continued on to the Greyhound section. She was a fine blonde, with a banging body but a lot of work.

"Let me take the window seat! Not in the mood to smell fried chicken and watermelon," she demanded when she saw Martin on the isle seat across from her. That was too close for her so she switched with her embarrassed boyfriend.

'Sorry,' the man mouthed and shook his head.

Martin again wondered if humanity was even worth saving. Especially when she launched into a tirade against blacks, Latinos, Asians and each kind of Indian. She saved Jews for last but got cut off before she really got started.

"Hey! I told you before that my mom is Orthodox Jew. A devout woman, so cut the shit!" he warned. She pouted for a moment but it wasn't long before that hate bubbled to the surface and spewed out of her mouth.

"Hitler had a point..." she blurted like she couldn't contain it.

"Fuck you Becky!" he decided and stood. The fasten seat belt sign was still on but the stewardess nodded understandingly. He took one of the other seats while she continued her rant.

"Finally!" Becky fussed when the bell chimed to remove seatbelts. She pushed her way down the aisle to be first in the bathroom. "Don't want any jheri curl juice on the seat!"

Becky relieved herself and checked her makeup in the mirror. She was as cute as when she walked in but just wanted to make the other passengers wait as long as possible. She heard the knock on the door she had been waiting for and opened her mouth to fuss but got cut off.

"It's Steven," he said and the door opened.

"Get in here!" Becky grinned wickedly and snatched him inside. This was an opportunity to kill two birds with one stone. She could further inconvenience the other passengers and get laid in the process.

"That will shut you up for a second!" Steven said when she squatted and inhaled the dick. She slurped, sucked and nodded in agreement. Once she had a rock hard dick she spit it out and turned around.

"Sssss!" Becky hissed when he slid up inside her from behind. She did like to piss him off on purpose since it made him pound the pussy with purpose.

"Mmhm, you, hateful, bitch!" Steve grunted and pounded. He was in a rush to get off before she did so he could leave her hanging. It was not to be when she began to quiver and curse. They both reached the same place at the same time.

"Not bad for a Jew boy," she snickered because she was so evil. Steven just laughed along with her since the joke was on her.

"Go on ahead. I need to clean up," he said and began to wash his dick as she stepped out. Becky wore a smug smirk all the way back to the seat until she saw Steven leaned against the window sleeping soundly.

"What the..." she wondered and spun just in time to see Lavar Burton leaving the restroom. Not the smooth, articulate Lavar, this was 'my name ain't Toby' Lavar. She almost screamed but the tingle in her vagina changed her mind. She shrugged her shoulders and sat her evil ass down for the rest of the flight.

Hours later he arrived in busy Mexico city.

Ricardo Blanca was a master weapon maker even before werewolves stole his family. They started with his sheep until they were depleted. Then they attacked his wife and children. Now they had an enemy for life who wished them dead. The perfect combination of rage and purpose when Kristine found him many moons ago.

Prince called ahead so Ricardo would be waiting on him when he arrived at the abandoned farm. His sharp senses picked up on snipers in each direction when he stepped out of the rental. He raised his hands in surrender even though bullets were like mosquitos to him. They left an itchy bump behind but otherwise harmless.

"Welcome!" Ricardo called out and the hidden guns lowered all around. !You look like your mother!"

"I hear that a lot," Prince said and shook the outstretched hand. He altered his face slightly to favor his mother's features since he could duplicate whoever he wanted.

"Come..." the host was saying until interrupted by a ghastly howl. Both looked up at the full moon overhead and Ricardo confirmed. "Werewolves."

"That's why I'm here," he nodded and followed him inside. As the number of vampires declined it shed light on the other non indigenous creatures on the planet. "To kill them all!"

"They are not very hard to kill. It's just so many of them! They turn hoards of people everywhere they go," he explained as they reached the armory. Prince immediately identified duplicates of some of the weapons he had made for his mother. A glass display case shined brilliantly under the laboratory lights and caught his attention.

"Silver," Prince nodded at the array of shiny swords and his favorite throwing stars. Ricardo went straight for a box of ammo and withdrew a round.

"It used to take five rounds of nine millimeter rounds to kill a mature werewolf," he said, holding up a much larger round.

"That's a fifty cal?" Prince acknowledged.

"Yeah, so now just one round will do it," Ricardo smiled, showing a mouthful of silver teeth. He picked up a star and flipped it into the heart of a full size werewolf poster.

"Hmp," his guest huffed and did the same. Except with enough velocity to split the first star in half.

"Werewolves are easy. Lycans, not so much," he said and moved on to the next display. He picked up a gel tipped bullet and handed it over.

"Silver shot?" Prince asked as he shook the round.

"Not fatal but enough rounds will knock one down. Then, cut the head off!" Ricardo added. "Your mother was working on a formula to kill them quicker, but she..."

"Died," he finished for him. It was clear from the look in the man's eyes he was one of many men who was in love with his mother. Most of the men who knew her were afflicted with the same ailment. A smile crossed his face in knowing only his father had the cure. That sparked a twinkle in his own eyes at a thought. "The cure!"

CHAPTER 14

"Hey baby! Hola mamacita! Dame un beso..." a slew of Mexican men whistled and flirted with the sexy blonde in the tiny red dress.

"As if!" she huffed and put a little more sway in her hips to advertise what they would never get. These dudes were standing in line to get inside the club and that was proof enough they were too basic for her.

She sashayed her fine ass right to the VIP entrance where she belonged. The bouncer never even saw her pretty face or blue. Those meaty breasts popping out the top of her dress demanded his full attention.

"Welcome to the Meet market!" he told the titties but they didn't respond. They did get the velvet rope pulled aside to grant free entry. He had instructions to let all beautiful women in free. Most came up missing after the night was over.

The blonde looked around the club flashing in the strobe lights and mirror balls. Couples gyrated on the dance floor as foreplay for the motel room after parties. Guys grinded erections on backsides as an audition for back shots later in the night.

That was beneath her so scrunched her face and lifted her nose above it. She was a VIP so she headed up to the VIP section. The tables of VIPs all called over for her attention so she had her pick. One night stands only last one night so she needed to choose wisely.

All the tables were loaded with bottles of bubbly and bubbly blondes, brunettes and redheads. One red head bobbed up and down under a table while a man leaned back and enjoyed throat. His boys groped other women in exchange for the free champagne. The expensive bottles came with free pussy which is really an excellent value.

The orgasm opened the man's eyes to see the blonde looking directly at him. His Eastern European features explained his friend's language. Euros still spent well in Mexico so they were balling out of control. The leader beckoned her over while shoving the red head aside. She couldn't protest since her mouth was filled with enough seeds to start a garden.

"Excuse me honey," she laughed as she squeezed by the woman and slid in next to the man.

"I am Orleg!" he said, pointing at himself.

"Karen," she said, doing the same. All heads turned to the American accent since most of the women in the Mexico city club were Mexican.

"America!" he cheered at the prospect of some good American pussy. Just like people think the grass is greener, those same people think the pussy is wetter or better somewhere else.

"Yes! Red white and pink," she teased and laughed at the looks on their faces. "I'll take all four of you back to my villa and rock your world!"

They had a brief discussion in Slovakian before heads began to nod. A wad of euros was tossed on the table to cover the bill and they pulled the white girl out of the club. The bouncer shook his head in mourning since she just left with four werewolves.

A limo ride later they arrived at a secluded villa and entered the gate. Karen led them all inside and up to the bedroom. They were here to fuck so the men quickly stripped. Now there were four dicks in the room pointing at the lone woman.

"Guess I better strip too..." she said and pulled the dress over her head. Now there were five dicks as she turned into he, him, Prince.

"What the fuck!" one demanded in his native tongue on behold of all.

"The one!" Prince replied and pulled two swords as the men morphed to wolves and attacked. An acrobatic flip and swipe of the blade cut the threat in half as two wolves lost their heads.

The leader lunged forward fangs first. Prince thrust a sword so far down his throat it touched his rib cage. A mighty grunt and thrust split the beast nearly in two. The last wolf had seen enough and leapt through the window. It landed fifty feet away and began to run full speed.

The werewolf looked back several times as it galloped away. It slowed down some distance later when he didn't see the threat behind him. Only because he was looking in the wrong direction. He finally looked up just in time to see a wolf like him. Except the wings that is. The flying wolf swooped in and scooped it off it's four paws.

A howl from above lit up the world below as the talons dug deeper into the flailing wolf. Falling from that height would prove fatal but that was literally the least of it's worries. The beast talons finally met in the middle of the wolf's body. A quick snatch pulled the werewolf into pieces. He rained down below to feed the stray dogs and cats of the city.

Tonight was the first time he hunted werewolves but it would not be the last. Next up was the big game, lycans.

"Hmmm?" Prince wondered as he perused through Kenyatta's computer through a backdoor he created.

The nerdy genius had a bad habit of flossing in the nerdy groups and online chats. He spoke in riddles but Prince spoke that and read between the lines. This guy was working for the lycans and needed to be killed. A better thought prolonged his life when Prince managed to hack into his computers.

"Nice," he nodded at the devices he manufactured to kill both species. Then paused to wonder, "Why?"

He got his answer when he came across Arrax and Rajeem. Brothers of the same mother, yet from different species. They were the key to eradicating both species from the planet. He decided they would be last and kept an eye on them. First things from first and he needed to try out some of these lycan killing devices Kenyatta came up with.

"He must have read Yolo..." Prince laughed when he came up with the DC 2000 like contraption. It worked though so he made a couple of his own. Now it was time to try it in real time.

Prince enjoyed flying but Brazil was a bit far so he chartered a private jet. The TSA frowned on guns, swords and DC 2000s so flying private was the only option. The long flight gave him time to read up more on his targets.

"Drink sir?" the pretty flight attendant asked as she buzzed around the cabin. It was her duty but she also wanted some attention from the handsome passenger. Prince had worn a Latin appearance since a black man flying private to Brazil would be remembered more. He planned to make a mess that would send a message.

"No thank you," Prince replied without looking up. Instead he looked down to avoid temptation but that's where her panties landed. He looked up just as she released two plump breasts from her bra. He just shook his head and pulled her on top of him.

The long flight was made a lot shorter with the beautiful woman riding his dick along the way. She ended up falling asleep in his lap so he had to wake her up when they landed.

"Here's my number..." she said as he exited the plane.

"For what?" Prince asked and titled his head curiously at the name and number on the paper.

"So you can call me silly!" she laughed, assuming he was joking. She planted a kiss on his cheek and slid the paper into his pocket. That's where it would stay.

"What's silly is giving me your body before giving me your name," he said to himself and collected his bags. A waiting car took him to the rented house and rented car he booked ahead. Once inside he showered the sex away and changed. Clothes and appearances and it was time to hunt.

"The Meet market," Prince said with a snarl as he arrived. There was no sign above the door but he was in the know and knew how to find them. The hot spot was spreading quickly around the world so it wouldn't be long until they reached the states.

Some of the foreign locations were lawless and species could feed right there on the spot. A fire would consume the corpses in the morning and they would move on to the next location. The smell of death greeted him as soon as he walked inside,

The presence of vampires tingled his senses but he was hunting bigger game tonight. He followed his senses to see a female vampire making out with an unsuspecting Brazilian man. Seeing the wide eyed look of excitement in his eyes made his head shake. Fool or not he was human and his mission was to save their species.

"What are you doing with my wife!" Prince growled hotly in the man's face. He looked more disappointed than scared since sexy women like this never gave him the time of day.

"I'm sorry! I, yeah, I..." he stammered as he looked down at his hand under her dress. No way to explain that so he took off. The woman just shook her head at the spectacle since he just volunteered to be her meal.

"I love a man who takes charge!" she purred and patted the now vacant spot next her in the booth.

"I take what I want..." he said, accepting the seat and replacing the hand under her dress.

"So do I..." she said and ran her tongue along his thick jugular vein. Prince adjusted his skin to allow her fangs to penetrate so they wouldn't break.

He smiled when he felt the fangs go in and then again when he felt her flinch. She knew instantly that she was in trouble but there was nothing she could do about it. Prince's skin and vein clamped down and held her in place. He wrapped her into a death grip as his venomous blood entered her mouth.

"You know you done fucked up right?" he chuckled like the cop in Menace to Society. She knew it too when she began to sizzle from the inside out. Her organs and cells collapsed when his blood coursed through her. Seconds later she was reduced to a pile of ash on the seat.

That was fun but it wasn't why he was here. He was here to hunt lycans and spotted a couple walking out of the door with a couple of women. The combination of hard liquor and high heels made one wobble but her date caught her.

"Easy there," he laughed and continued out of the club.

Prince stepped out a second later as their car pulled away. He could have followed in his own car but what fun was that. Instead he looked up towards the sky and took flight. The upward look looked cool but served a practical purpose after flying into a street sign.

He watched from above as the car navigated the city streets until reaching a hotel. He waited until they were all inside the window before crashing the party. Literally since he crashed through the window. The women screamed loudly at the intrusion.

"Wait, y'all are here with lycans who plan to eat you, and coming through a window scares you?" Prince asked incredibly.

The lycans had no idea who he was but he was clearly a threat. He didn't smell like a werewolf but he clearly was not human. Either way they both morphed and bared fangs and claws. Prince tilted his head at the women and their delayed reaction. It took another second before they both screamed.

"That's more like it..." he called after them as they made their escape through the door. The lycans both pounced from both sides. Prince was armed but didn't pull his weapons. This was his first encounter with this species so he wanted to see what they were working with.

"Uh-oh," he gasped when they hurled him back out the same window he crashed into. They both took the first step to follow but it wasn't necessary.

"Don't run now! The party is just getting started," he said from behind them. The lycans shared a 'WTF' glance but

Prince was gone by the time they looked back up. When they did they felt a coil wrap around their necks. There was no time to process when they snapped shut and removed their heads.

"Shit..." he fussed at the mess left behind. Werewolves change back to human form when killed but lycans obviously don't. He couldn't leave the room littered with headless monsters. Someone had to clean this up and he was someone.

CHAPTER 15

Prince killed as much and as many werewolves and lycans as he could on his own. Vampires had withdrawn underground and were killing each other to get stronger so they could fight him. All the species had hundreds of years of headstart and he realized he needed help.

Once Kenyatta turned into a hybrid monster Prince decided to get the help he needed. He had something he knew the brothers wanted, but they would have to be convinced to join him. So he killed them...

"Well?" Rajeem asked, pulling his brother from his thoughts. His mind was made up but he wanted to hear from his big brother first. Four hundred years is a long time to go without good advice.

"A cure tho..." Arrax repeated. Those words had been ringing in his head since the man left. A cure meant the chance to live a normal life and die a natural death. His mind flashed back to Hakeem's severed head coming through the windshield. An unnatural death if ever there was one.

"Well?" he asked again since his brother went back into his own head. He did have an opinion so he voiced it. "Dude has a point. This world is for humans."

"And we're going to help him give it back to them," Arrax decided. Supernatural species had caused more than enough carnage on a planet that didn't belong to them.

"And be brothers again. Like before," Rajeem added hopefully. He lost some of that hope when his brother began to shake his head.

"No, not like before. We'll be
brothers like never before!" Arrax defined and hugged his brother for the first time in hundreds of years.

"Awwwwe!" Nandi moaned and rushed over to make it a group hug. She looked over to the bedroom door and pouted. "Wish my sister would hurry back to life so we can all be together!"

"Soon," Arrax said and extracted himself from the hug. "But in the meantime...
"

"Let's go kill some shit!" Rajeem said and let his fangs hang when he smiled.

"Let's!" Nandi agreed and made a few chomps
in the air.

"Yeah, no, I was talking about us.The guys, boys night out," Arrax corrected but Nandi's head kept shaking from side to side. "Or you can come with."

"Yeah, best to let women win," the little brother advised the older.

"I see," Arrax nodded. He was the leader so he led the tribe out for battle. There was a pack of lycans he knew here in Kensington.

Rich and privileged who preyed on the poor and underprivileged from the poor and underprivileged areas of the city. They were already on Arrax's list but now he had more reason to eradicate them. Not to mention there were ten of them. More than Arrax could handle by himself. Now he had help.

"They will know we're coming," Rajeem offered while they rode over to the castle the group held for hundreds of years.

"That's why you'll be in chains," Arrax replied, giving his plans.

"Ooh I like chains! And whips!" Nandi laughed. The brothers didn't so she straightened her face. "I'm listening."

"Good. I'll bring you in as captives. Once we're inside, we attack!" he said plainly.

Rajeem snarled jovially at the chance to kill lycans in general, and especially with his brother. He knew of a pack of wolves in nearby Ireland and added them to the list. Tonight would be a busy night.

Arrax felt several sets of eyes on them as they winded down the winding road to the castle. Rajeem's head whipped from side to side as he smelled his enemies from every direction. They were completely surrounded by the time they reached the entrance.

"It's Arrax!" one shouted and lowered his silver sword. He was the only one who disarmed at the mention of their leader's name.

"And wolves!" Another declared and took an offensive posture. Both Rajeem and Nandi reeled in fear they didn't feel. They would usually feel the mere presence of silver being near but thanks to the shot from Prince's gun they didn't.

"My prisoners! Let's take them inside for Sheba," Arrax snapped. Mention of the queen of this particular castle took the puff from the puffed up chest.

"Oh, alright," he agreed and lowered his sword. He did check the heavy chains securing the prisoners before giving the nod that lowered the drawbridge.

"One way in," Rajeem noticed aloud.

"And no way out," Nandi snarled. They realized Arrax had miscalculated the amount of lycans when double the ten met them in the queens court.

"Arrax dear!" the queen stood, cheered and threw her arms open.

"Sheba," he r

eplied and took her offer of a hug. He pressed himself against her big bosom while plotting his attack.

"He hit that," Rajeem nodded.

"I'm gonna hit that next," Nandi growled on behalf of her sister.

"I brought a present!" Arrax announced and pointed to his captives.

"You mean another present?" Sheba asked and gripped his crotch. That's when the plan went out the castle window.

"Oh hell naw!" Nandi snapped and transformed. She shed the chains as easily as Clark Kent coming out of his clothing.

"Women!" the brothers said simultaneously and morphed as well.

"It's a trap!" the leery one from the gate declared. He had been on a particularly high alert since lycans were coming up dead all.

"I like traps..." Sheba declared and backed away from Arrax as he transformed. A clap of her hands brought another twenty lycans out.

"Not enough!" Arrax growled as he kept on growing past

the normal size of a lycan. A moment later there were three hybrids standing ten feet tall.

"Let's get it then!" Sheba said and morphed. The forty on three battle was completely lopsided. For the lycans that is.

The tribe fully explored their new powers in an explosion of violence. Skin, limbs and blood filled the air as the lycans were cut down. Their own swords were used against them to remove their heads. Even fatal wounds become nonfatal if the heads aren't separated from the body.

Once the smoke and red mist of blood settled only the tribe was left standing. They had officially joined the war

.

"Well, look who's up!" Arrax cheered when Harlow blinked awake. She looked around to get her bearings after being dead in between species. It took a few seconds before things started to make sense to her. She remembered more as she looked around.

"What is that noise?" Harlow wondered of the rhythmic pounding like someone beating a drum.

"My brother and your sister expressing their love," was the best way he could put it.

"Well, we're in love..." she reminded since she woke up horny.

"Of course! But, you've been dead, so let's hit the shower," he laughed and helped her up.

Arrax gave her a head start to get herself together before joining her. A few minutes later he joined her under the steamy water. After a few minutes of foreplay they added to the sexual symphony ringing throughout the house.

Squishing and splashing added with the bumping and grinding until all parties were satisfied. Once everyone wrapped up the loving they met in the living room to plan their next attack. Rajeem knew of some werewolves in London but they had discovered the location of a vampire from the castle.

"When can I..." Harlow asked anxiously. Nandi caught her drift and clapped her hands eagerly.

"Do it!" her sister urged and sat up to watch. Harlow looked at Arrax and got the nod.

"OK, OK, OK!" she said but nothing happened. "How do I change?"

"You have to want to. Just want it..." Arrax said and began to morph until his head touched the ceiling.

Harlow gave up trying to force it and simply wanted it. She felt herself beginning to change her species until she was nearly as tall as Arrax. She too was a modified version changed by the combined DNA of the brothers.

"Yay!" Nandi cheered as her big sister took swipes and bites with her new fangs and claws.

"Let's go try this shit out on those vampires," Rajeem suggested. He had been around them in the various Meet markets of the world but never went fang to fang with them.

"Let's..."

Nandi agreed. The moon had just replaced the sun and dark traded with light.

"There's a coven of witches over in Scotland as well," Arrax announced his recent discovery. "Led by a witch and warlock couple named Samantha and Darrin."

"Nandi and I can wait..." Harlow began and paused to

recall where she knew those names from. "Like, Bewitched? The TV show?"

"We used to love that show when we were growing up!" Nandi cheered and tried to wiggle her nose. She couldn't so she transformed her nose into her snout and wiggled that.

"We didn't have TVs growing up," Rajeem remembered.

"Only because it wasn't invented," Arrax said and took back control of the briefing. "Rajeem and I will handle the wolves. You ladies destroy the coven."

"Kill all the witches and warlocks," Rajeem added. They learned to pull the bad plants out from the root so they couldn't grow back ever again. "The vampires are ours!"

"Best to catch them during the day," one of them said. They all looked around to see which one did until Prince slowly visualized before their eyes. One second there was nothing and the next second he was there.

"I wanna do that!" Nandi pleaded to Rajeem.

"Shit, me too!" he seconded while Arrax seemed perturbed.

"Can't knock nigga?" he snapped. It wasn't the intrusion so much as the vulnerability. He was used to being atop the food chain but this guy made him feel like food. A snack actually since he could turn invisible.

"My bad," Prince said and raised his hands in surrender. He could read minds and understood the man's dilemma. No one ever wants to be shown up at any time and especially not in front of their woman. "So, I gauge by the mess you made at the castle that you're in?"

"We're in, as long as you keep your end of the bargain. The cure," Arrax bargained.

"Cure? Cure for what?" Harlow wanted to know. She had just become supercharged and wasn't ready to go back to normal.

"For dying," Arrax said. "This world belongs to humans. We're going to help give it back. Then go back to being humans ourselves."

"Awe man," Harlow pouted but that would be the end of the protest. She vividly remembered the few minutes she spent alone while everyone she loved lay dead. Remembered wanting to die with them, so she would live with them.

"Good. I brought some weapons..." Prince said, disappeared then reappeared with the weapons. "To kill vampires."

"Can we do that?" Harlow asked and tried to make herself disappear. She only got disappointed since lycans didn't have that ability.

"We are weapons to kill vampires!" Rajeem spoke up on behalf of the tribe.

"Yeah well..." Prince said and let the smirk finish the thought. Everyone knew he was a lycan and werewolf killer so it didn't need to be said. "I sensed around a hundred vampires in the hall."

"No problem," Arrax declared and stood. He finally picked up one of the weapons and acted like he wasn't impressed. Only because he didn't know what it was. It looked like a street sweeper shotgun with the round drum underneath.

"Wooden stakes. Fifty rounds per second," Prince said proudly. It was his mother's design but he had it modified.

"Dope!" Rajeem said grabbing the other since there were only two. "None for you!"

"Yeah, no I'm faster!" Prince said. They were about to find out once they headed out of the apartment.

Prince watched as the men kissed and hugged their women before departing. He stuck his chest out to confirm his decision not to love again until this was over. Rajeem and Nandi made out hot and heavy while their older siblings shared pecks and loving words. They placed their women in the car and waited until they pulled off before coming back to their own vehicle.

"Not riding?" Arrax asked when Prince didn't move towards the car.

"Nah, why ride when you can fly," Prince said and lifted slowly off the ground. "See you guys there..."

"I kinda like that guy!" Rajeem admit
ed. Arrax did too but wasn't going to admit it.

CHAPTER 16

The brothers knew the witches were light work for the women but the huge pack of wolves could be a problem. They didn't need to be worrying about their women while trying to kill the wolves. They traveled by separate vehicles and agreed to meet back at the apartment once the deeds were done.

"You know they gave us the light work don't you," Harlow pouted as she watched the rolling English countryside roll by the window.

"Men are the protectors and maintainers of women," Nandi shrugged as she repeated what she heard Rajeem say on more than one occasion.

"That's the same thing Arrax said!" She replied. The rest of the ride was spent reflecting on the wisdom the men imparted on their women. Their sensitive noses announced their arrival before the GPS said so.

"Smells like?" Nandi asked when she couldn't identify the aroma.

"Eye of newt and frog balls probably," Harlow laughed as

she envisioned a large cauldron bubbling over a fire with witches standing over, stirring with long spoons.

"Let's add some witches and warlocks to that pot!" Nandi growled and put the car in park. They analyzed the large barn for a moment before approaching. There were no cameras or security to be seen. Suddenly the door opened as they approached.

"You ladies here for the coven?" A happy red head semi slurred from the stout served inside.

"Uh, yeah?" Harlow answered on their behalf. The woman swung the door open to invite them in and the smell they smelled hit them in the face.

"Witches smoke weed?" Nandi asked but Harlow didn't know since she had never met a witch before. Her lips twisted dubiously as they entered.

"I think we've been sent on a wild goose chase!" Harlow surmised with a snarl. She could see her handsome man's handsome smile at the diversion.

"Well, we're here," Nandi shrugged and stepped fully inside. There was a cauldron alright but it was being used as a bong. People dressed as witches and warlocks all took big tokes off the weed in between sips of the dark stout on tap.

"I guess that's Samantha and Darrin huh?" Harlow asked and nodded towards the couple sitting on thrones. They passed a smoking cup of liquid back and forth while overseeing the festivities.

"That's my jam!" Nandi sang when the DJ mixed in a Doobie Daddie song. Her sister just shook her head when she rushed the dancefloor and began to dance.

Harlow wasn't in the mood for dancing so she moseyed around to see what she could see. Her sharp hearing could hear multiple conversations around the room. She laughed at the corny lines a would-be warlock was spitting in a wannabe witches ear. It worked and he led her away for a quickie. She turned her hearing towards the pretenders on the throne to listen in to what they were saying beneath the smiles pasted on their pasty faces.

"Nice turn out," she said and he agreed.

"Yes. Now we need to select a few for sacrifice," Darrin replied while looking around. A smile spread on his face when his eyes came across Harlow's. "And there she is."

"I do believe that is!" Samantha exclaimed and cast a spell. Harlow felt her feet pick up and drop as they carried her to the throne. "How would you like to have eternal life?"

"That's why we're here," Harlow answered and nodded towards Nandi shaking her booty on the dancefloor.

"American!" the couple cheered as if they won a prize. Nandi looked up and Samantha cast yet another spell that brought her near as well. She walked over as if in a trance and stood by her sister.

"They offered eternal life," Harlow relayed. Nandi's head shook up and down in agreement.

"That's why we're here," she said under the same spell. The couple stood and led the sisters into an adjoining room.

The smell of real blood now drowned out the weed being smoked next door. Both knew the magic was real and they were a real witch and warlock. They led the way to the blood soaked altar at the front of the room and selected knives.

"Lay down..." Samantha demanded since they were under her spell. Both sisters knelt and bowed their heads to be chopped off at the neck.

The wicked witch and warlock lifted their blades to do the deed, then everything change in an instant. The submitted women suddenly changed and grew. Samantha and Darrin's eyes grew and filled with fear as the women morphed into beast.

"What, what are you!" Darrin demanded as the knife fell from his hand.

"Hungry!" Nandi announced and took his head off. She lolled her head back and wolfed his head down her throat.

Samantha lifted her hands to cast a spell but Harlow bit them off. She did the next best thing and turned to run but that takes legs. Harlow bit them off next. Samantha could only scream when the creature snatched her up by the torso. Harlow followed Nandi into the main room with the woman in her mouth.

Nandi let out a roar that made the needle jump off the record. They had everyone's full attention as they took the center of the room. Some faces smiled in awe of the realistic display. Others grimaced in worry because it was too real- istic not to be real. Nandi transformed back into her human form for a speech.

"This world is for humans! God created it for humanity! Not witches, not warlocks! You can stay human and live! Or..." She said and turned to her sister.

The crowd moaned, screamed and grimaced when Harlow closed her jaws on the squirming, screaming woman. The crunch of bone sang out over the gasps and screams before the woman was cut in half. There was a brief pause before everyone scrambled for the doors. A few seconds later it was just to two sisters remaining. And the bong.

"Here we go," Arrax said after the GPS announced they were.

"These creatures sure can party!" Rajeem said of the packed parking lot and traces of music leaking from the hall. Prince landed right in front of them and opened the door for Arrax.

"Valet?" Arrax quipped and tossed him the keys.

"No tip?" Prince chuckled before going deadly serious. He head whipped towards the building and tilted. "Something is wrong? There were at least a hundred..."

The brothers looked at each other as Prince took off towards the door. Both shrugged and followed him inside with the guns raised for battle. Except the battle had already taken place.

"The fuck?" Prince asked of the hundred or more empty vampire shells. A bunch of empty civilians lay around the large room as well.

"Good question?" Arrax asked and took his side. "What could have done this?"

"Lycans?" Rajeem wondered since his kind didn't leave meat on the bone.

"Vampires, but who? Why?" Prince asked but only he could answer. There was only one answer and it eased from his mouth. "To get stronger. Regular vampires grow stronger from killing other vampires. They don't usually but..."

"But there's some strong ass vampire on the loose!" Arrax determined. And he was right.

"Yeah," he agreed and wondered who. He had been killing vampires across the globe and this was the third time he came across a scene like this. If it was the same vampire responsible then Arrax was right. This was one strong ass vampire.

"Well, there's some sheep out back so..." Rajeem said on his way out back to eat the sheep. Mary may have had a little lamb but Rajeem ate ten.

"Why us?" Arrax asked once they were alone again.

"Because of your humanity. It was you who urged your

kind not to feed on humans," he replied quickly. Which quickly led to Arrax's next question.

"Why my brother then?" he asked because Rajeem was clearly a savage at one point.

"The same," Prince said to his surprise. The surprised look on Arrax's face spurred an explanation. "I went to destroy a lycan feeding center. Your brother beat me to it. He saved a woman and nursed her back to life. I looked deep enough to find out you were brothers. Once you worked out your beef I knew you two would make a good team."

"Four. Us four. We're a tribe," Arrax declared to Prince's nodding head. It stopped when a thought held it in place.

"Five. The five of us," he decided. "We're the tribe!"

"I'm ready for a nap!" Rajeem announced as he returned, rubbing his belly. Prince and Arrax just shook their heads and laughed.

"Why don't I ride back with you guys?" Prince suggested since they were bonding.

"Shit you can have my seat if I can fly!" Rajeem said wishfully. He still hasn't learned to be careful what he wished for.

CHAPTER 17

"Guess I could hang out for a bit..." Prince thought aloud after the brothers went to their women. He may have given up on love for the time being but still loved some good loving from time to time. This was one of those times so he hit a club.

"Come right in..." the burly bouncer announced like it was his own idea when Prince approached the VIP entrance of the club.

"Why thank you kind sir," he replied with a smirk since had given him the command to let him in.

Now that he was inside he looked around at the menu. This wasn't one of those menus people have to read. No, this menu was shaking ass and titties on the dancefloor. All like any menu they made the items seem more attractive.

Martin wasn't sure if he was in the mood for black, white or other until he saw her. A pretty Bangladeshi woman with jet black hair and brown skin. The skin tight dress showed off her curves like a street sign. No trace of panty lines meant she wasn't wearing any. The big nipple prints said she wasn't wearing a bra either.

He had made his choice so he made his move. The man next to her at the bar suddenly lost interest and walked away in the middle of his proposition of various positions. She tilted her head curiously then blew her breath into her hand to make sure that wasn't the problem.

"What's the verdict?" Prince asked as he took the recently vacated bar stool next to her. He equated mind control to get sexual favors as sexual abuse. So he turned it off and turned on the charm.

"Smells like pussy!" she laughed.

"Does it taste like pussy?" he asked and leaned forward for a taste. Only halfway though so she had to meet him in the middle. She did and their tongues twirled in each other's mouth for a moment.

"Does it?" she asked when they pulled back and locked eyes.

"I'll have to taste yours to be sure?" he offered and she accepted by extending her hand. Prince took the hand and stood. He turned to escort her into several positions until something stopped him dead in his tracks. Someone actually.

"What?" the woman reeled since he looked like he was seeing a ghost. He was since he was looking directly at his dead mother across the club.

"Mother?" he wondered and began to wander in that direction. He rubbed his eyes to make sure they weren't deceiving him. They were because when they next opened it was Melcina staring back at him. She laughed louder than the techno music booming through the speakers. Prince was faster than sound so he crossed the room in a blur and snatched the woman by her throat.

"What the hell are you doing!" the woman's date

demanded. Prince looked up at the total stranger straining to stay alive under his death grip. Her face turned blue and her feet kicked in the air.

"I, I thought? I, I'm sorry!" he blurted and rushed for the door. He just made it to the sidewalk when a hand grabbed his arm. He spun for battle but this wasn't that type of battle.

"Wait! I like to get choked!" the pretty, Bangladeshi lady purred.

"I..." Prince stammered. He was confused about the visions but good Bangladeshi pussy is very effective against confusion. "Let's ride!"

And ride they did. First in the 2021 Range Rover Prince was driving. Then she rode the dick like a bank robber on a horse with the posse behind her. The only thing to do was pop one of those nipples in his mouth and hold on.

Prince's body was here with her but his mind was a million miles away. He ran through the night he killed Melcina to see what he missed. His head shook from side to side with the nipple in his mouth and made the woman moan.

She was coming while he was going, over every possible scenario. His vision was too sharp not to see what he saw but that was impossible. The woman howled as a final orgasm rocked her world. She keeled over off the dick and began to snore. Prince barely noticed and kept on trying to make sense of the implausible.

"As salaamu alaykum wa rahmatullah..." Arrax said to each side as he and Rajeem wrapped up their morning prayer. They hadn't missed a single prayer after seeing their places in the hell fire. A second chance at life meant a chance not to go to that fire.

"Just beautiful!" Harlow gushed as she and Nandi watched from the rear. Neither understood the words he recited but reveled in its beauty. They made it a point to watch the men pray their five daily prayers. Even when Arrax would slip out of bed to shower and pray in the middle of the night. She would lay there and listen.

"We should eat," Rajeem offered. The women nodded in agreement. Arrax nodded too but had another idea in mind.

"We should get married," he stated plainly. Harlow looked confused for a moment and ran through what else those words could mean. They couldn't mean anything else so she lost it.

"OK! Let's go!" she shouted and headed for the door. The woman always dated the wrong men for the wrong reasons so this was the first proposal she had received. It was also the first time she had been in love so she wasted no time.

"OK, but we should get dressed first?" Arrax reminded and nodded down at her nightgown.

"Oh yeah!" she agreed and rushed off. Meanwhile, Nandi practically stared a hole into the side of Rajeem's head.

"What?" he said when he felt the heat of her gaze.

"What? Get dressed is what! We are getting married too!" she growled. Rajeem knew the difference between a command and a request so he stood to follow the command. They were mates for life since they died together already. Now they would live together as husband and wife. Wolf man and wolf woman.

"You asking me, or..." Rajeem began to ask but by the look on her clearly she was telling him. "Is black OK?"

"Mmhm," she hummed and joined her sister in getting dressed.

"Never thought I'd see this day," Harlow said in muted disbelief.

"Why? You're beautiful!" her sister assured her. She certainly didn't think this day would come when she was held captive in the hoe house. Definitely not when she occasionally awoke in the breeding facility.

"I was a bit of a hoe," Harlow laughed. It was a bit of an exaggeration but she used men as a means to an end. Sometimes it was for information, others just to get her rocks off. Nothing that would have led to this.

"No. You're my big sister and you're beautiful!" Nandi assured her and hugged her neck. The pretty girls had an ugly cry and resumed getting dressed. A half hour later all parties met in the living room and nodded in agreement with how nice they all looked.

"Let's ride," Arrax said and led the way from the unit. His brother joined him in the front seat while the women rode behind them.

Their leader had taken the lead and scheduled a small service at a nearby mosque. Four people walked inside but two couples exited. They were all smiles until they saw someone sitting on the hood of their vehicle. He was a stranger at first, then morphed into someone very familiar.

"Bravo!" Prince clapped and stood. He saw the question forming on Arrax's face so he went on and answered. "Kenyatta put trackers in you both. I tapped into them a while ago."

"But why are you here?" Arrax asked since there was nothing he could do about Kenyatta now.

"Because we have work to do. It's worse than I thought. More, dangerous," he revealed even though he wasn't sure what exactly he was dealing with.

"Well, we have some consummating to do. So we'll holla back!" Nandi insisted.

"Enjoy yourselves. We leave for Egypt in a month. Someone has called all remaining vampires for a summit," Prince said. It was just like the meeting they just came across and found nothing but dead vampires. Prince left that part off and dissipated into smoke and disappeared.

"You sure we can't do that?" Harlow moaned. Arrax just shook his head but wished he had that type of power. His head shook the thought away a split second later. Mortality is what he wanted most. To live a simple life and die a simple death.

Arrax was still in command of the lycans since none of the lycans got the chance to spread the word about his new mission. As such he ordered as many as he could to Afghanistan. They would meet in the same system of caves that sheltered Osama bin laden so well, for so long.

Rajeem still had to pull with his own kind since he was so well known to be so brutal. It was easier to do what he asked than to fight him. He summoned them all to neighboring Pakistan the following week.

Killing them in bits and bites was not only taking longer but word was spreading that tribes were being killed. If either species went underground they would be harder to find and kill. They booked a private jet to carry the array of werewolf and lycan killing weapons. Deadly devices created by Kenyatta, Harold, and Ricardo. None deadlier than the tribe created by Prince.

"You're really not going to invite Prince?" Rajeem asked as the flight lifted off the runway.

"For what? He knows our every move," Arrax reminded since they both had tracking devices in them. The revelation came as a bit of a relief since he wondered how he kept two steps ahead of them.

"I see..." Rajeem said and pointed out the window. There was Prince flying alongside. He smiled, waved and sped off.

"No one likes a show off!" Arrax grumbled and pulled down the shade. Nandi pulled Rajeem up from his seat and drug him down the aisle to the bathroom. They had more consummating to do.

"You asking me, or telling..." he was saying when she snatched him inside.

"Newly weds," Harlow laughed.

"Like us!" her new husband reminded and pulled her into his lap. The bathroom provided some privacy but the thrill of getting caught added to the excitement.

"Naughty boy!" Harlow cooed and shimmied out of her tight jeans. She was as ready as he was by the time they undressed from the waist down. She reached down and wriggled him inside of her.

They twirled their tongues in each other's mouths as she slid slowly down his shaft. Then slowly back up, down, up, down, Then threw her hips into overdrive and rocked the whole plane. The pilot came over the intercom to apologize about the turbulence, but it was the turbulent sex rocking the plane.

"No wonder they couldn't find bin laden!" Arrax announced when they reached the cavernous system of caves in Afghanistan.

"They didn't want to find bin laden!" Rajeem corrected like someone with first hand knowledge. The same knowledge that led to bin laden being allegedly killed rather than captured. Then allegedly thrown in the sea rather than buried. He didn't believe it for a second.

"I hear them..." Harlow mentioned. She was still getting used to having super senses and didn't know they were still a few miles from the meeting place. "I smell them."

"I smell blood. Human blood!" Arrax said and transformed. The rest of the tribe transformed after him and caught up. Four blurs sped towards the campgrounds on the ground while another jetted overhead.

"Just a little snack?" a lycan in human form pleaded as he peered through the bars of a large cage holding a large number of Afghan civilians. Over a thousand souls gathered as food for the meeting.

"Wait til Arrax comes. He gets the pick of the litter. Grab a sheep to hold you ov..." another lycan was saying until a huge eagle swooped in and took him away. Once the bird reached a few hundred feet above the ground it shredded the lycan with its talons.

'I wish I could do that!' Arrax thought as he watched the airborne carnage. He couldn't but he could kill many lycans on the ground so he attacked.

"We're under attack!" a man screamed as he transformed into lycan.

Arrax's battle plan was to work from the perimeter, inward. Killing every creature they came across. Prince was the perfect compliment to the plan when he dive bombed into the center of the battle. He could transform into any creature in the creation but chose to mimic the rest of the tribe.

The regular lycans were no match for the supercharged beast created by Prince's formula. Arrax and the crew were equal parts werewolf, lycan and deadly. Thousands of lycans answered the call. None would live to tell about it.

CHAPTER 18

"And they thought the Taliban were the bad guys!" Harlow said as her husband and brother in law released the Afghan prisoners.

"Taliban means students. All we know about them is what their enemy reports," Nandi reminded. She had traveled enough with Rajeem to know Western media tells the story the way they want. Not necessarily the truth.

"Shukran! Jazakallah khairan!" the grateful people said as they filed out of the cramped cages.

"Afwan. Afwan," Arrax replied to each with a slight bow. Prince watched and nodded at being right about these two. They had good in them.

The tribe loaded the prisoners back into the same transports that brought them here, then drove them back to their villages. They then used those same vehicles to make the trek over to Pakistan. Killing werewolves was a bit easier than lycans but the weapons were much more effective.

"Nice turn out," Rajeem nodded as they neared the soccer

stadium chosen for the event. Once again a host of humans were collected as food to feast on after the meeting.

"Makes our work easier," Nandi said and rubbed his hand. This second chance was actually a third for her. She was ready to get it over so they could enjoy real life.

"Yeah..." Rajeem agreed but she wasn't sure to what since he was obviously elsewhere. She just patted his hand once more since she was down for whatever, wherever, whenever.

Prince rode with Arrax and Harlow in total silence. They even muted their thoughts so he couldn't intrude. Arrax had things on his mind but pushed them out to collect later. The end was rushing toward them as quickly as they were rushing towards this next battle.

Prince had tuned out the internal antenna that picks up people's thoughts to respect their privacy. He actually respected the man even more. He still had to do what needed to be done because this world was created for mankind and jinn. Not werewolves, lycans, vampires, witches, warlocks or whatever else. He had to do what he had to do and that was all to it.

An elaborate array of guns and silver bullets rattled in the back of the truck. Along with silver swords and throwing stars meant they were fighting this battle in human form. They still had their super strength even without transforming.

"So, what's the plan?" Prince asked when the first sign announcing the proximity of the soccer stadium passed by.

"Kill them all," he shrugged, then elaborated. "We'll use the silver nitrate grenades on the perimeter to make sure no one escapes. They'll have humans, so we can't just bomb the place."

"Yeah?" Prince asked and tilted his head since the thought

of bombing the joint had just crossed his mind. A moment later he shook it off as the coincidence it was. Saving human life was their whole agenda. There would be no collateral damage.

The truck went silent again when the stadium came into view. It wasn't long until a lone wolf let out a loud howl.

"Shit!" Rajeem fussed since he spoke that language well. He grabbed the phone but the report was evident before he got to report it. His plan went out the window when wolves began filing out of the stadium. Prince went out the window as well and flew straight up into the air. "Don't say it!"

"I wasn't!" Harlow laughed. She wasn't going to say it but they both wished they could do that. They did the next best thing and hopped out of the truck. They selected weapons and took aim at the rushing wolves.

Werewolves were used to getting shot so the guns didn't scare them. Only silver bullets had any effect on them and most people didn't have them. They quickly found out the tribe wasn't most people. They were barely people at all.

Sounds of yelps joined the growls and howls from the werewolves once the silver bullets began flying. Wolves went flying like bowling pins from strike after strike.

Rajeem tossed the grenades that emitted the fine silver threads that shredded any werewolf it came into contact with. His strategically placed explosions corralled the wolves back toward the gunfire.

Prince transformed into a huge bull and charged. Werewolves hung from his horns as he trampled through their pack. His hooves killed as many as his horns.

"Let's get the civilians!" Harlow announced. Nandi covered her back with automatic gunfire as they charged.

"Oh no you don't!" Nandi exclaimed and swung her

sword. Her sister tilted her head curiously at the human head tumbling in the air. She quickly realized some of the wolves transformed back into human form to escape the onslaught.

"We can smell, you!" Harlow caught on and lopped off another head.

The gunfire went from fully automatic to sporadic as the targets decreased. All the wolves lay dead or dying on the battlefield. Now all that was left was a silver bullet to the brain of any survivors. Nandi and Harlow followed up by removing the heads. There would be no coming back from this.

The werewolves joined lycans on the list of the extinct. All that was left was the vampires.

"You know he's going to kill us once this is over don't you?" Rajeem asked in their native Wolof since whispering was useless around werewolves and lycans.

"Yeah, most likely," Arrax agreed. He had thought about the same outcome himself.

"What are we going to do about it?" he asked, ready to follow his big brother's lead. The moment of silence belied the fact that Arrax had already made up his mind for himself.

"Nothing," he replied. "We had a second chance and we did good deeds. In sha Allah it'll be enough."

"To see ummi?" Rajeem wondered with wonderment in his eyes at the prospect of seeing his beloved mother once again.

"God willing," Arrax repeated in English this time. His brother nodded his head and accepted their fate. They had been at war with each other for hundreds of years but had a chance to die as brothers. That was fine by him.

"What was that about?" Nandi asked since she had seen the seriousness in the brother's faces when they spoke. Plus she had tuned in with her super sharp hearing but didn't understand Wolof.

"The future!" He cheered as if the future was brilliantly lit instead of the bleakness he had accepted.

"As long as we're together..." She replied and left the sentence open because it didn't matter how it finished. As long as they were together.

"Well, let's go kill some vampires so we go home!" Harlow announced to all. She wasn't sure where home would be but as long as they were all together it didn't matter. Her home was with her tribe.

"Let's!" Arrax said and led the way. They would fly ahead and meet Prince in Egypt, or so they thought.

"Sup," Prince greeted as he boarded the jet.

"What, not flying?" Arrax quipped as he took a seat. He would surely fly like Superman if he had that power.

"Of course. Flying with the tribe," he said as a matter of fact. Arrax mulled that over for a second before speaking up again.

"A tribe only has one leader," he advised and carefully watched his features for deceit.

"And you are that leader. I asked for your help. Because I need you," Prince said to him, then turned to them and continued. "I need all of you. I can't do this by myself."

"We're with you," Rajeem nodded in agreement. He had accepted his brother's leadership and was glad Prince did too.

"We knocked a dent in both werewolves and lycans!" Arrax added. They had too over the last few months. The species was completely wiped off the face of the earth.

"This will be the largest gathering of vampires, ever,"

Prince said without a trace of the worry that was worrying the shit out of him. Not even his father had the authority to call a summit. Only Katrina or her husband Vladimir wielded that type of power.

'And my parents killed them both!' he thought. The thought put a snarl on his face but the rest of the tribe was busy hugging, kissing and loving to catch it.

The fact that someone had the juice to summon the entire vampire nation was troubling. Vampires are normally territorial. Living alone or in small groups. This was an army and every army had a general. Like the werewolves and lycans the tribe had knocked a dent into their numbers. Killing this gathering of blood suckers would wipe out the species.

Prince looked over at the two couples with mixed emotions. He was a part of their tribe but they were part of the problem. Supernatural beings who didn't belong on this planet. He knew what had to be done and would do it when the time came.

"Good old Egypt!" Arrax announced and inhaled the rich aroma of one of his favorite countries. The food was some of the best on the planet even though he ate the sheep before being seasoned and cooked.

"Man, I haven't been here since..." Rajeem said and paused to think. Arrax didn't need to think about when because he remembered the what.

"Nineteen seventy eight. You ate the Hizbul-shaitan brotherhood," he reminded. This time he smiled because the upstart terrorist group needed to be eaten.

"Ah yes. It Tastes like chicken," Rajeem recalled. "I like my people raw like sex!"

"I'm not eating people," Harlow grimaced, grossed out by the thought. The banter continued until they neared the venue. Then turned deadly silent with the deadly seriousness of the situation.

"Here," Prince said and held out his hand.

"What is it?" Arrax asked before moving to take the four syringes in his hand.

"What I promised you," he said and turned away. Arrax accepted the offering and tucked them away. "The leader must die. Even if it costs our life, he must die!"

"Yeah," Arrax sighed and retreated to his woman.

"You OK baby?" Harlow wondered as her man drifted inside of his head. So deep in thought he could only nod. To speak would have been a lie. He was not OK. Their book of life had flipped to the last page.

"Thousands!" Prince said when he felt the strong presence of vampires. It grew stronger with each inch they inched towards the arena. All entrances and exits were blocked off to control the throngs entering.

"We got thousands of rounds!" Rajeem snarled. He was armed with the rapid fire wooden stake device and with the shits.

"Plus these!" Arrax added of the bullets Prince gave him for last resort. They looked similar to the ones that killed them before.

"One way in," Nandi stated the obvious. They filed into the venue with the hordes of undead.

"No way out," Arrax added as he looked around. He noticed several sets of eyes on the tribe and wondered if the element of surprise had been lost.

"We're coming out the same way we walked in," Harlow said and lifted her chin triumphantly. She spun sharply when the sound of chains securing the doors rippled through the arena.

"Showtime!" Prince growled when a spotlight beamed in the middle of the floor. The attendees backed away for the star of the show. The head had to be killed, so the body will die. Arrax and the tribe spread out with their weapons and waited for his signal.

Prince waded through the crowd to get a glimpse of the leader. A large black cat purred and rubbed against his leg in passing. It had his full attention as it slinked into the spotlight and began to grow. Prince's eyes grew along with the cat. It went from black cat to black panther to black woman. Not just any black woman.

"Mom?" Prince asked as his long departed mother smiled at him. A smile began to form but didn't get a chance to fully develop before it changed again. This one was just as unbelievable as the first. "Melcina? I, I killed you!"

"No, you killed her..." Melcina said and nodded towards the woman standing next to him. Prince turned and saw Melcina standing next to him.

"Argh!" he grunted and lopped her head off. The head rolled right next to another Melcina. He lifted the sword again to see he was surrounded by Melcinas. "Attack!"

The tribe began firing the wooden stakes into the hearts of the many Melcinas. There were a thousand of them but they had thousands of rounds. Soon they were running on the bodies of the fallen while fighting the ones still standing. Prince was only concerned with one.

Melcina took flight but Prince was right behind her. She stopped in midair and with a wave of her hand all the other vampires fell dead. Their souls shot up from the ground and entered her. She grew even larger as she slowly descended back to the earth.

"How?" Martin asked when he confronted her back on the ground.

"Because, I'm you.." she laughed and transformed into him. Martin's head tilted to the side as he looked directly at himself.

"The fuck..." Arrax grunted as he aimed his weapon back and forth between the two.

"Him! Shoot him!" they both shouted and pointed at the other. "Not me, him!"

"Left!" Rajeem announced. He and Nandi pointed their weapons at the left Prince while Arrax and Harlow took aim at the one on the right. They all fired at once but both Prince's took off into the air. The fight became even when they went through the ceiling and landed on the roof.

"How?" the real Prince asked once more.

"I've had your blood since you were a baby. Wasn't sure if I would ever need it. Especially when your mom refused to turn me," she explained.

"Because this world is for humans! Look how much destruction you've caused!" he shouted and pointed through the hole at all the dead bodies. "And Ximena! I loved her!"

"Yeah," Melcina pouted remorsefully, then smiled. "She was delicious!"

Prince growled and transformed into a large lion. Melcina laughed and did the same and the battle was on. Fur and blood flew as the lions clawed and bit each other. Both fell through the same hole landed on the ground with a thud and continued fighting.

All aimed but none fired since no one could tell which one was Martin. What was clear was that both lions were killing each other. Arrax loaded the bullets of last resort and went back and forth between the two. It had to end here so he made a decision.

"Fuck it!" he said and fired. He alternated the six shots between the two lions until the gun clicked empty.

"Uh-oh!" Rajeem exclaimed when both beasts turned towards them. Both bared their huge fangs and roared with enough ferocity to blow the women's hair like a blow dryer. They lifted their weapons once more as both lions took a step. Then it exploded.

The tribe was ready to shoot as chunks of both lions fell like confetti. They expected them to merge and come back to life at any moment, but they didn't. Arrax turned to make sure they didn't. He came back with the explosive charges and tossed them around the arena.

"Let's go!" he shouted and led the charge. They barely cleared the venue when a mighty roar lifted them off their feet. The explosion tossed them a hundred more feet before dropping them back to earth.

The tribe stood there for an hour with their guns ready. It was only then they realized that the Prince wasn't coming back.

"It's over!" Nandi cheered and hugged her husband. Rajeem wasn't so sure so he turned to his brother.

"Not quite..." Arrax said and produced the syringes. He and Rajeem picked up their tacit conversation from before. They surmised Prince intended to kill them all once the deed was done. Still, he handed them to each. He was right, this world belonged to humans.

"Ummi," Rajeem said and sighed. To see his mother again made dying dear to him so he plunged the needle into his thick skin and pressed the plunger.

"Oh no you don't!" Nandi declared and did the same. She wasn't letting him out of her sight, even in death.

Arrax watched the two drop dead and still inserted the

needle into his arm. He locked eyes with Harlow who did the same. They shared a last smile and depressed the plungers. They joined the rest of the tribe on the ground and in death.

The End

EPILOGUE

"I got my period!" Nandi shouted as she rushed from the bathroom. She was a new woman when they awoke from the dead as mortals once again. Life was new and so was this. "Do you know what that means?"

"Head for a week?" Rajeem guessed hopefully. Nandi just shook her head and twisted her lips. He wasn't necessarily wrong, but that's not what she was talking about.

"If I can bleed I can breed silly!" she explained. Becoming a werewolf had fixed more than her spine. Being reborn from the dead gave her new life and new womb.

"I can still get head tho right?" he asked and got popped.

"What he say now sis?" Harlow laughed as she and Arrax joined them in the garden of their shared compound. The Haitian hillside made for a perfect place to live a normal life and die a normal death.

"Could be anything knowing this one!" Arrax added and inhaled. He hadn't enjoyed the fresh air as a mortal in four hundred years. It seemed sweeter than he could remember. A new chance at life was even sweeter. As was the new life growing inside of Harlow.

A large black bird swooped through the patio and hovered for a moment. Just long enough to have its presence known, then flew off again.

"You think"...Rajeem asked.

I'm sure!" Arrax nodded and watched it disappear into the son. Prince was still alive and still the one.

The tribe went back to their conversation and mortal lives. Life was good since they were still alive. Even though they would one day die a mortal death.

Unless Prince needed their help again one day...

THE LAST 48

By

Sa'id Salaam

7:00 AM Friday

"Hmp!" Marlo fussed as she looked at herself in the full length mirror. The 38-year-old woman could easily pass for ten years younger. It had been twenty years since she'd given birth to her one and only child and that was plenty of time to get her body back tight and right, just like it was.

It wasn't vanity that made her huff indignantly, it was the date. Today was her son Thad's twentieth birthday. It was also the day his killer was due to be released from prison.

"Two years for killing my child. Seven hundred and twenty days for taking my Thaddeus away from me." she said for the seven hundred and twentieth time. Not a day had gone by that she didn't mourn the loss of her only child or curse his killer.

The part that made it even worse was that she actually knew his killer. She'd practically raised him since he lived right across the street in her southwest Atlanta neighborhood.

She'd helped raise Carlos aka Lil' Los since his mother, Nita, hadn't been that interested in being a mother. However, she did know all the latest dances and could roll a blunt like nobody's business, she just sucked at parenting. Physically Nita was a year older than Marlo, but mentally she was twenty years her junior. In another dose of insult to injury the woman had been turning her nose up at her since after the "incident". That's what they called her son's murder since Carlos claimed it was an accident. Several friends who'd witnessed or heard about it after the fact said the two close friends had fallen out over a-sixteen-year-old named Dana.

Marlo knew the girl was trouble since the first time she saw the half-naked teen prancing around the neighborhood. Back then she'd sure hoped she would have picked Carlos over Thad, but found the girl at her house daily. Several times she'd came home from work to the smell of sex hovering in the air and the two looking guilty. She'd also seen how flirtatious the girl was with other men, including her own.

155

Back then she was dating a fellow school teacher named William. He was definitely marriage material, but the stress of her losing her child pushed him away. Marlo was slapped in the face yet again when Dana popped up knocked up shortly after Thad died. She'd claimed from day one that the child was Thad's since he was her first. Carlos was her second and she counted at least three more before the girl had started showing, and she'd counted quite a few more once she'd given birth to her grandson. Once Thad and Carlos were gone she was circulated throughout the hood like a STD.

Marlo verified paternity the first chance she got by offering to watch the baby. The young girl wanted to turn up so always needed someone to watch him. Marlo watched him in the car seat as she drove straight to a DNA lab. It confirmed what she could tell just by looking at the infant. She was now the proud grandmother of a child whose name she could not pronounce from a young woman she could not stand.

She almost wondered what her Thaddeus saw in the hoochie since she wasn't particularly pretty. Her skin was pockmarked and her wisp of hair was usually gelled down to her scalp. She didn't wear many clothes and it was obvious as to why when she heard the girl was slinging coochie around like a Frisbee. According to people with knowledge she'd driven a wedge between the close friends when Thaddeus dumped her. Thad dropped her and found a more suitable girlfriend. One who wore whole shorts and shirts and had a whole future with a whole scholarship. The hood rat didn't like being snubbed and so began talking to Carlos to spite him. During pillow talk, she said Thaddeus was talking shit about Carlos. Talking shit is a capital offence in the hood because he was dead a day later.

Two days later Carlos was arrested. Meanwhile, Dana just moved on to the next man. Another friend of her sons who told her that Carlos bragged about intentionally killing her son. The *hearsay was inadmissible in court and plus he refused to testify. That too was a capital offence that got your ass gunned down in southwest Atl, or any hood for that matter.*

The prosecutor pointed out the fact that Thad was no saint. He was no demon either, but had once caught petty weed and possession of gun charges. Another cruel twist since it was Carlos's gun but Thaddeus took the charge that would have sent his friend to prison. A good defense lawyer could have taken the arrest and run with it. He'd offered the plea deal rather than risk letting him get off Scott free. Marlo reluctantly agreed, mainly because she literally could not bear to see the person who killed her son every day. With him living directly across the street she would been forced to.

Forced to see him laughing and smiling while her son decayed in a box six feet under the earth. Then that nasty little Dana over there with him. Probably having her grandson over there too breathing loud pack and listening to loud music.

"Oh God!" Marlo wailed and felt her knees buckle. Luckily a strong pair of hands caught her and held her up. Just like they'd done when she'd almost collapsed in the courtroom.

"Whoa," Deputy John Jenkins said when he swooped in and caught her. He had been the bailiff in the court when Carlos took his plea. They made eye contact a few times during the process but it wasn't the time or place for a love connection.

William had just left her citing he couldn't deal with her depression. He got ghost and left her to deal with it on her own. John had caught her before she hit the floor now just like he did then. Carlos's was the last case of the day so he'd ended up driving her home. The act of chivalry led to a sex act on the sofa. A furious bout of sex with torn hosiery and panties pulled aside. The pleasure eased her pain for as long as he was inside of her. Somehow they kept it going two years later. She was in a lot of pain. The peace officer made her feel good and safe by laying plenty of pipe and giving her a pistol to protect herself. A dainty little nine millimeter that packed enough power to kill.

"You know what today is?" she moaned and sank into his embrace.

"Mmhm," he hummed because he didn't. He was going to guess birthday but wasn't quite sure. Perhaps they'd reached some sort of anniversary, but he wasn't as committed as she was. She may have been in a relationship with him, but he still liked to spread love and dick throughout the city.

"Today is the day that boy comes home. Two years and he's home free while Thaddeus is still gone and ain't never coming back!" she wailed. "How am I supposed to look at that boy every damn day? Huh?"

"Just ignore him. Don't say nothing to him. Don't look at him. You have to get over it," he suggested with a frustrated sigh. He just knew he could get a little action before going on duty. Her tears said otherwise so he'd have to get off during his shift.

"Then-then if it was really a so-called "accident" then why he ain't never said sorry? Ain't you supposed to be sorry when you have an accident?" she pleaded.

"Yeah." he said dryly hoping it was over since they both had work. There would be no sex, so he looked at his watch and announced the time.

8:15 AM

Deputy Jenkins was now assigned to a car since he got in trouble working in the court house. His dick slinging ways got him caught on camera getting a blowjob by a civilian. Being back in a vehicle suit him just fine since he got to be in contact with female fugitives.

"You go to jail, or suck a dick and go home?" he laughed, practicing his favorite line. It worked at least once a day, sometimes twice. His record was three but today's lineup looked even more

promising. A bad check and credit card ring had been discovered and warrants had been issued.

Jenkins followed his GPS to a west side apartment complex and parked in front of a unit. He tried to sound out the multiple syllable name but it was a mouthful. Ghetto enough to hopefully give her a mouthful. A few young dealers scrambled when they saw the uniform. Deputies seldom make drug arrest but they weren't taking any chances.

A skinny dopefiend saw the cop and made beeline in his direction. She knew on duty cops were the biggest tricks so she made her pitch.

"Tryna get yo dick sucked-ed?" she asked with a wink and an extra ed.

"Sure am." he laughed and rang the doorbell. The crack addict sucked her yellow teeth and slinked away.

"Who!" a deep voice boomed from behind the door. The cop unhooked his gun holster as the heavy footsteps came closer. Serving warrants can be extremely dangerous because no one likes to go to jail. The door was snatched open by a four hundred pound woman holding a pound cake in her hand.

"Shanateriza Jackson?" he barked coming pretty close to nailing the name on the first try. It was close enough that she didn't correct him.

"Huh?" she nodded identifying herself. She glanced around the living room full of merchandise stolen with stolen credit cards and bad checks.

"I have a warrant for your arrest. Who else is in the house?" he asked walking in on her. She had no choice but to back up so he could enter.

"Nobody," she pouted, sticking her lip out. The cop looked her up and down, undeterred by her large size.

"Well, you have two choices. You can go to jail or suck some dick?" he explained. Ten minutes later he emerged from the apartment feeling relaxed and slightly sleepy. "One down, three more to go for the record."

9:00 AM

"Hey, Marlo girl!" Marlo's coworker Janice greeted as she entered the teachers' lounge. She was bubbly from today being Friday and two days away from these bad ass kids.

"Hey girl," Marlo replied with a sigh and sipped her coffee. Her watched beeped signaling she was due in class but couldn't find the strength to get up.

"Girl, what's wrong with you! That cop had you up all night, handcuffed to your headboard?" she laughed.

"Naw," Marlo said shaking her head. Last night was one of the rare nights they didn't have sex. He'd tried, but she was just not in the mood for love or sex.

"Well, let's hang out this weekend. It's been a minute," she offered hoping to cheer her up from whatever had her down.

"Okay," she sighed even though she had no desire to go anywhere or do anything except curl up and die. In a few hours Carlos would be a free man.

12:30 PM

"Al Hamdulillah, the brother Hasan finna bounce up out this peace!" Abdul-Hakim cheered as he entered the brother's cell.

"Yeah," Hasan croaked unsurely as he sorted out his belongings. He had amassed quite a bit of food and property since his mother kept his books full. "I'm leaving my books to the brothers."

"We good akhi. Take them with you so you can continue to study. And remember, first stop..."

"The masjid, I know, akhi," he said. In the couple of years he'd been in prison he'd seen plenty of brothers go home and revert back to the streets as soon as they hit the streets. Mainly because their first stop wasn't the masjid or mosque as it's also called.

In fact only 3 out of 10 'chain gang' Muslims actually stay on the path once they're released. That's because 3 out of ten joined the ranks of the Muslims for reasons other than faith. Faith never entered their heart in the first place. Most were just plain scared and wanted the safety that comes with numbers. Prison is a dangerous place that can turn men into mice or women or make them pretend to be Muslims.

Some know from day one that they're faking while some don't realize until they get released from the stress that is prison. Then their same vices and bad habits overtake them and they're right back in prison.

"You okay, my brother?" Abdul-Hakim laughed to lighten the moment. He could literally see his temples jump from the conflict within. He'd seen the reality of release shake many men in his many years of incarceration. He remembered when Carlos first came in with that city swag until one of the gangs put the press on him. He quickly came to the Muslims and joined the ranks. In prison you have to join something and the Muslims were the easiest group to join. They didn't jump you in like the gangs.

"Yeah I..." he began but was cut off when his name was called. "Welp, I'm out!"

"Now stay out! Don't fall off and come back, bruh." the brother said and threw open his arms to embrace him.

"I ain't never coming back! Believe that!" he insisted but didn't say 'In sha Allah'. A Muslim never says anything about something to come without saying 'God willing'. Abdul-Hakim thought about that as he watched his brother leave the dorm, to leave the prison.

"Don't come back!" the officer barked as he processed Hasan out of the prison. He could tell someone cared about the kid since he had a check for a couple hundred dollars from his books. Most prisoners only get the $35 bucks the state gives upon release. It didn't matter if you just did thirty five years, all the state of Georgia had for you was $35 bucks.

"I ain't never coming back!" he shot back once again without saying 'God willing'. He like most inmates hated this mean old officer. They claimed he hated young guys. It was partially true because he hated seeing young black men throwing their youths away in prison. Running around the prison with their pants sagging, ripping and running like it was a joke.

"God willing," the officer added since Christians say 'God willing' as well. "Just keep that kufi on your head and do what you supposed to do!"

1:00 PM

Hasan nodded and signed his papers to officially become a free man. He deliberately held his breath so his next one would be as a free man. A van drove him to the bus station for the two hour ride back to his beloved city of Atlanta. For most of the ride he quietly recited melodic verses from the Qur'an. Halfway to the city he looked at his reflection in the window. He pulled his kufi off just to check his waves. Somehow the kufi never made it back onto his head. He was Hasan Muwakil when he boarded that bus but two hours later Lil Los stepped off in Atlanta.

1:38 PM

"Whew!" Deputy Jenkins exclaimed as blow job number two came to an explosive end. So far he was batting a thousand since no one wanted to go to jail. Especially on a Friday since there would be no seeing a judge until Monday. That meant a weekend stuck in the dirty, nasty, dangerous Fulton county jail.

Mmhm," Diamonique huffed sarcastically. She knew she had some all-star head and didn't like being coerced out of it. She did have some fly shit from the hot cards so she acquiesced and sucked him off. "Told you don't come in my mouth!"

"Yeah, but that would have defeated the purpose," he chuckled. The real joke is that the quick fix only lasted a day or so. The unserved warrants go back into a pile to be served again another day. He could get them again and get his dick sucked again or it could go to another deputy and they were going to jail.

The cop probably needed professional help for his sexual addiction because he could and would do this all day.

"So, I'm good?" the wanted fugitive wanted to know.

"Okay, I guess," he shrugged assuming she meant her oral skills. "Catch you later."

2:15 PM

"There goes my baby!" Nita cheered when Carlos stepped from the bus and looked around. He smiled brightly and braced himself for a strong embrace.

"Hey, Mama!" he laughed as she hugged all the air from his body. He could smell weed smoke just below the splash of perfume she'd used to mask it. He looked towards Broad Street knowing the masjid was there. Right there, two blocks away. A custom in Islam is to stop by the mosque and pray when returning from a journey. Not a day went by that some returning Muslim stopped by to practice that ritual, except today that is.

"Look at you! Let's go get you something to eat! Shit, I'm hungry too!" she announced as the munchies kicked in from smoking weed.

"Fish Supreme?" he asked hopefully. In his defense that's some good ass fish but he was already abandoning his adopted religion.

"Hell yeah!" she cheered and pulled him to the car where a man waited behind the wheel.

"Sup?" the driver greeted with a head nod as they reached the car.

"Catfish, this my son Carlos, Carlos, Catfish," she said making the formal introduction. As formal as could be with a grown man named after a fish species.

"Sup," he greeted back and winced from the weed smoke hovering on the cars headliner. It had been two years since he smoked but it was a daily habit before that. He thought about intoxicants being forbidden in Islam when Catfish passed a smoldering blunt into the back seat. He debated for a whole second and a half before accepting it.

"Welcome home, baby!" Nita cheered when her son took a deep pull on the blunt despite him having to check in with probation on Monday morning. Most prisoners who get released on a weekend end up turning up all weekend then turning up dirty when they get pissed tested on Monday. Parole ends up being a weekend pass for many a drug addict. Habitual pot heads are just as much drug addicts as cocaine and heroin users.

2:45 PM

Catfish pulled into the parking lot of a Fish Supreme near the house. He looked at both mama and son snoring from the strong weed and shook his head. He reached over and groped a titty to wake her up but it didn't work. Nita had been fucked in her sleep before so a simple titty squeeze didn't even register.

"Nita! Say, Nita!" he called out while shaking her. The noise and movement woke Carlos instantly. Sudden noises would forever put him on high alert after what he'd experienced in prison.

"What's up?" he asked, leaning forward just as his mother stretched her arms and wiped a line of drool from her chin.

"We finna eat is what's up!" Catfish replied and hopped out. Nita and Carlos got out and followed him inside.

"You ain't shit!" Nita griped when her boyfriend made a separate order and paid for it. "You got money son?"

"I ain't cashed my check yet," he said almost apologetically.

"Don't worry, it's my treat," she sang and dug under her wife beater and into her bra. She produced a ten dollar bill moist from the heat and sweat of her softball sized breast.

"Thanks. Let me get a fish supreme, hush puppies and a sweet tea!" he said rubbing his hands together deviously. His mother shook her head and laughed then placed the order.

"I'm finna run next door and cash my check," he said since it would be a couple of minutes before the fish came out of the hot grease.

"Grab me a forty. And some scraw-berry blunt wraps!" she said, aiming to get back what she was spending on the meal.

"Kay, Mama" he said and hit the door. The liquor store shared space in the same strip mall so it was a short walk. Again he was reminded of Islam's prohibition on intoxicants as he dug his mother's favorite malt liquor from a tub of ice. He grabbed another for himself and approached the counter.

"Got ID?" the clerk said asking about the check, not alcohol sale. He would sell liquor to a two year old but wasn't getting stuck on no bad check.

"Uh, yeah," Carlos replied digging out his prison issue identification card. Ironically, he kept it in his pocket size Qur'an. He ignored the contradiction and handed it over. The clerk held it up to compare faces and nodded.

"How long you did?" he asked, guessing it was nowhere near the ten years he'd once did since the kid was only 20.

"Two," Carlos said with a proud nod since doing a bid is a badge of honor in the hood. The clerk chuckled at the 'skid bid' and completed the transaction. He shook his head know-ingly at the kid as he walked out. He knew if he was buying alcohol and weed with his 'coming home' check he was going back.

"You ain't get me one?" Catfish frowned seeing he only brought two bottles.

"Nigga, you ain't buy us no food, but you want a free beer! Boy, stop!" Nita fussed on behalf of her son.

"Tryna front in front ya son," he pouted like men raised by their mama's tend to do. They can be downright bitchy and bitch-like at times. They want and expect every woman to cater to and coddle them like their mama does.

"Boy, stop," she repeated and patted his hand to comfort him. "I'll let you have some of mine. 'Kay?"

Carlos twisted his lips at the display. He'd always viewed his mother as just a mother but now realized she was a woman. Islam came back to mind and reminded him that men are the protectors and maintainers of women. He failed in that and left his mother to the likes of Catfish. It was cool because he was home now. He dreamed of teaching his mother about Islam and imagined her covering, fasting and praying. Now wasn't a good time so he would just wait 'til later. Once he had her alone, once the drugs and alcohol wore off.

"You ready, baby?" Nita cooed snapping him back to the present. Both he and Catfish replied in the affirmative, assuming she meant them.

3:15 PM

"What the...?" deputy Jenkins wondered at his next fugitive. The name Raynard Starr was normal enough but all the aliases raised his eyebrows and curiosity. "Raynisha, Starrleta, Denisha."

He frowned up at the mug shots in different names and genders. He was a handsome man when he wanted to be but also a pretty, pretty girl as well. A warrant is a warrant so he shrugged his shoulders and hopped out of the car. He adjusted his utility belt like Batman and walked towards the door.

"Who?" a woman's voice called as the sound of heels click clicking on the tile floors sang backup. The sounds of the lock being unlocked prevented him from replying since he would see who was ringing as soon as he opened the door. "Ooh!"

"Raynard Starr?" he asked looking the man in full drag up and down. A tank top showed off the brand new breast he bought from cashing hot checks. He looked sexy even though he had a dick under the short skirt he wore.

"He not here. I'm Raynisha," he said nodding to make the cop believe it.

"That's fine cuz I have a warrant for that name too," he said, nodding so he would believe him too. He stepped up and inside forcing Raynard to step back or get stepped on.

"You really gotta lock me up?" he pleaded in falsetto, batting his false lashes. He saw the way the cop locked in on the manmade breast and did a little shimmy to show them off. This certainly wouldn't be his first cop.

"Bruh, are you trying to seduce me?" Jenkins scoffed indignantly.

"I most certainly am!" he said turning on his well-rehearsed feminine charm.

3:35 PM

"Three down. One more for the record!" he said when he left the apartment twenty minutes later. A record is a record so he shrugged his shoulders and got back into his car. He should have driven himself to some rehab for sex addicts. Instead he drove towards trouble.

Twenty minutes after that he arrived at yet another fugitive's last known address and got out. The pretty little white girl made his dick jump in anticipation. Some white girl head would be the perfect way to close out a record setting day. He still planned to spend a night with Marlo to make up for what he missed last night.

"Yes?" Becky asked and flipped her good hair as she answered the door. She almost expected the police to show up after using what she knew was a stolen card. She was glad her lawyer dad was out with her lawyer mom so they wouldn't find out.

"Rebecca Shaw?" he asked using his official deputy sheriff voice. As professional as he tried to be his eyes still scanned her from blonde hair to pink toes.

"Yes?" she demanded taken aback by the flirtatious gawk. She now wished her lawyer dad and lawyer mom were home. "Can I help you?"

"No, but I might be able to help you. Actually, you can help yourself. I have a warrant for your arrest on charges of bank fraud. I would hate for you to have to spend all weekend in that nasty jail."

"So would I. I need to call my dad!" she whined.

"You'll get a call once you get to the jail," he advised and removed his cuffs. "Unless... you want to work it out?"

"Can I!?" she pleaded and opened her mouth to ask how but he reached for his zipper to explain. The girl's tears didn't stop her from doing what she had to do so she could stay free.

Her tears didn't stop the cop from thoroughly enjoying some white girl head. They certainly didn't stop the surveillance cameras from recording the entire incident including the sound. Not just the slurping and moans from the blow job in progress but the crime that led up to it as well.

4:35 PM

Carlos let out a lonely sigh when he looked at the

mosque as they drove past it on Cascade. He heard the call to prayer and saw the brothers entering and knew it was time to pray. His mind screamed to Catfish to pull over so he could go pray but Catfish could barely read text so he certainly couldn't read his mind. When he opened his mouth the taste of beer closed it back. He couldn't pray while inebriated.

"We home!" Nita cheered when the driver barreled into the driveway. The first thing Carlos saw was his old hooptie sitting on cinder blocks. Nita's car was beside it badly in need of being washed. Although not quite as bad as the grass needed to be cut. Proof Catfish didn't do much around the house except the plumbing. He laid plenty of pipe and that was enough for Nita.

"What happened to my rims?" he asked cocking his head. At one point he would have killed or died for the huge chrome wheels. Now he was just curious since he planned to sell it and buy something more befitting of a Muslim. Wasting of wealth is a sin in Islam and big chrome rims were definitely a waste. There's nothing wrong with having nice things but extravagance is frowned upon. After all, spendthrifts are the brother of the devil.

"Ion know?" Nita said out her mouth but the guilt on her face was obvious. During rough times she sold them to get over the hump. At least she did put some of the money on his books. "Don't even worry 'bout them. I'll buy you some more!"

"Aight," he shrugged since he really didn't care. As soon as he stepped out of the car, his head was magnetically pulled across the street. His heart ached so much it made his knees buckle causing him to hold on to the car for support.

"That loud pack got 'em!" Catfish cheered since stuff like that was important to him. He could give a fuck about Syria,

Dow Jones, or global warming. His chief concern was getting high and getting laid.

"You okay, baby?" Nita asked genuinely concerned. She followed his eyes across the street and sighed. "I know, baby."

The trio made it inside and flopped on the sofa and chair. The beers were cracked open again and another blunt was put in the air. Carlos felt his eyes getting heavy and tried to fight. He was no match against the alcohol and strong weed; especially after being clean and sober for almost two years.

"Come on," Catfish said once he blinked himself to sleep. He was so use to dealing with baby mamas so he knew the best time to put his dick in them is as soon as the kid goes to sleep.

"Okay," Nita giggled and followed him down to her room. They stripped like it was a race and flopped naked on the bed.

"Suck a nigga dick or something?" he asked romantically.

"Eat a bitch out!" she shot back indignantly. He blew his breath in defeat and climbed on top of her. She reached down and guided him inside. As soon as he was in he began to hump rhythmically. Meanwhile in the living room, Carlos began to dream....

"I wonder what Thad doing?" Dana asked stifling a giggle. She loved seeing Carlos get jealous over her. She'd never been loved before so jealousy would have to do.

"What you asking 'bout him 'fo?" he shot back like she knew he would. Especially since they were naked on his bed making out.

"I was just asking! Dang!" she cooed and reached for his erection. She knew she was pregnant since she hadn't had a period since Thad's rubber broke. She was so smitten she put her whole hoe tendencies on pause and had no doubt it was his. He hit it a few times and moved on to the next girl. A cute, clean little thing who read books and spoke properly. She just couldn't understand why

he chose her over her when she was freaking him any way he wanted it.

"You like this, huh?" Carlos grunted as he humped away inside of her. He was glad she didn't make him wear a condom so he could feel the heat and liquidity first hand. Why would she since she couldn't get any more pregnant.

"Mmhm," she moaned and wiggled under him. He didn't last long in the young box that still had the elasticity that makes vaginas great. Misuse and abuse can leave one stretched out and useless like an old pair of socks that fall down around the ankles. She gave a kagle squeeze and it was a wrap.

"Argh! Mm, shit!" he cussed and fussed, making crazy faces while pumping her full of semen.

"Mm, Thaddeus. You got that good love," she moaned and squeezed a little more.

"Bitch, get the fuck up out my shit!" he demanded and snatched out. "Calling me by the next nigga name?"

"No, I didn't?" she whined, enjoying the show. It was all she could do not to laugh in his face at the look on his face. Her simple mother told her if a man won't whoop your ass he don't love you. She was trying to get him to show her some love.

"Thad told me you was hoe!" he shot back to heap some hurt to match his.

"And he told me you was lame!" she said reaching for her panties. The remark pouted his lips in disbelief.

"My nigga ain't said nothing like that!" he demanded hotly. As much as he looked up to Thaddeus he knew he wasn't insulting him to some neighborhood jump off.

"Yeah, he did!" she insisted since she saw she'd hit a nerve. "Said you a lame and yo mama is a hoe. Said she tried to give him some!"

He sank to his bed from the weight of the insults. He knew Nita was generous with her vagina but a hoe? His mother did always say how handsome Thad was? And he a lame? He wasn't as tall and muscular as his friend but, lame?

"I'm sorry, baby," she cooed and wrapped her arms around him from behind. Her warm, firm breast made him feel a little better in an instant. "He just jealous cuz he knowed I like you."

"Hmp?" he wondered trying to reconcile her words with reality. He tried to push up on her when she first moved into the hood but she was all over Thaddeus. Most girls did like the handsome athlete over him.

He was so deep in thought he didn't notice her come around and go down. The undeniable pleasure of a hot mouth killed all rational and reasoning. He leaned back and enjoyed the demonstration, while the seed of hate was sown in his heart.

8:00 PM

"Carlos, wake up baby!" Nita called, shaking his leg. He was actually relieved to be awakened from the dream since he knew what was going to happen next. He'd relived it so many times, like the radio playing the same song three times every hour. The dream of that day ruined many a night's sleep. He blinked his eyes when he registered she wasn't alone.

"Yeah, nigga! Get yo' ass up!" Mann laughed, kicking his foot. He was surrounded by Fresh and Hot Rod. The gang was all there except for Thad who would be forever late.

"Sup?" Carlos chuckled, seeing his friends. His watch began to beep to remind him it was once again time for prayer.

"Turn up, my nigga!" Hot Rod demanded, sticking a blunt in his face. He contemplated for a moment and made a decision. He would turn up and party tonight, then tomorrow he would make all his prayers and go to the mosque. Islam gave him peace and dignity instead of the chaos and humiliation of his former life.

"Yeah, my nigga!" Mann cheered when he hit the weed. He passed him a tall can of cheap beer to chase it down with.

"And we finna hit the club!" Fresh added and handed him a couple of name brand bags.

"Wha...?" he asked seeing Nita looking on happily as he dug in the bags and found clothes and tennis shoes.

"I tole them your sizes!" she said so he would know her contribution.

"Something for yo' pocket," Mann said, handing him a roll of cash. The couple hundred looked like more since it was street money consisting of ones, fives, tens and wrapped by twenties.

"Me too!" Hot Rod said pressing a bag of bagged crack so he could get his hustle back on like before he left. They meant well and thought they were being helpful in their own ghetto ways.

He accepted the drugs even though he vowed never to go back to the trap. Abdul-Hakim had arranged a job for him with one of the brothers. All he had to do was meet him at the masjid. Most of the brothers had their own businesses or hustles and would gladly give him some work. All he had to do was show up.

"Tomorrow," he thought to himself, because he didn't want to disappoint his friends. He didn't understand that whenever a person truly intends to change, his old friends become his new enemies. Anything else is like taking a bath and putting dirty clothes back on.

"Um, okay," he acquiesced. He left his mom and friends smoking weed as he went to take a shower. Carlos took the ritual bathing Muslims call a ghuls. Except it's to purify for worship, not the club. Instead he was off to do everything contrary to Islam like Isis or Al Qaeda. Again, he vowed it would just be one night. After all, he owed his mama and friends for making his short stay in prison as comfortable as a stay in prison can be. As bad as confinement is it's even worse being hungry.

Most people believe what they see in prison movies where the inmates go through the chow line while heaping spoonfuls of hot food is heaped on the tray. The truth of the matter is that Georgia prisons feed grown men like small children. Worse even since there is no lunch on Friday, Saturday and Sunday. Dinner chow is called from four to five PM and that's a long time until breakfast again the next morning.

"Just one night. Gonna get up for Fajr in the morning, then hit the masjid," he nodded as he washed. He stepped out, dried and got fresh in his new clothes. He'd hoped all the weed and alcohol had been consumed by the time he got back but no such luck.

"Let mama blow you a gun!" Nita cheered when her son returned. She put the lit end of the blunt in her mouth and began to blow. It was just like old times when he leaned into the steady stream of smoke and inhaled.

"Yeah, my nigga!" Hot Rod shouted when he began taking it up his nostrils. He took his place when he fell away full of smoke. Nita had enough breath to fill his lungs as well.

"What club y'all finna hit?" Nita asked offhanded, hoping for an invite. Catfish got ghost after he got off so she wouldn't mind hanging out with them. It was either that or the local American Legion and gin with some old player trying to lay his old pipe.

"We finna hit that 231!" Mann cheered but left out the part about her coming with. Once the weed was depleted they hit the door to hit the club.

10:00 PM

Marlo heard the laughter outside and got up to investigate. She grabbed her pistol from her purse and went to her front door. The black burglar bars allowed her to stand in her doorway and see without being seen. Her breathing seemed to pause when she saw Carlos smiling from ear to ear. She thought he looked directly at her, although he couldn't see her and laughed heartily. Now her heart stopped as well seeing he thought it was funny.

"My baby is gone and you laughing. It's joke huh? A game!" she spat too angry for tears.

"Who you talking to?" John asked as he came out of the bathroom.

"No one," she said and quickly closed the door. He tried to come over but she blocked him with hug and kiss.

"Mmhm," he nodded knowingly at the distraction. If she wanted to offer some sex he would take it. He kissed her all the way down the hall and into her bedroom.

Marlo quickly stripped and climbed on the bed while John took his time. He marveled down at her firm body and shook his head. Had he been the marrying type he would have married her. Just for her looks alone even though everything else about her was a plus as well. The well liked, well respected teacher had dibs on the next assistant principal position that came available. In the meanwhile, she assumed her favorite position on the bed.

John Jenkins was a handsome man but she still preferred not to have to look at him during sex so she put her face down and ass up. She would never admit it, but she really didn't like him. She liked being alone even less so she put up with him.

He came around her and entered her doggy style, like the dog that he was. and began to hunch. Luckily her body responded to the sex act because her mind was a million miles away. Figuratively speaking since it was really just across the street. Her body rocked from the movement but all she saw when she closed her eyes was Carlos's smiling face. It was the same face he'd made when she used to make cookies for them. He would devour the treat then hug her with all he had. Cookies and love didn't get at home.

"Hmp!" she huffed seeing his mocking smile tonight. John began to hiss and moan behind her signaling that the end was near. She hated she'd missed what was usually some pretty good sex. Tonight all she could see was that smile. That mocking, sarcastic, *I killed your son and only got two years, so take that* smile.

"Mmm, Shit! Whew!" John exclaimed as he filled his condom. He slumped over on her back and fought for breath. The best orgasms damn near kill a man, and this was a good one.

"Okay," she said and rolled away. He fell beside her and began to blink and yawn. Snores soon followed but she was wide awake with her thoughts. She fought her sleep knowing one of those haunting nightmares was waiting on her like Freddie Kruger.

11:00 PM

"Where all the hoes?" Hot Rod asked seeing mostly dudes in the line in front of the club.

"Hoes get in free before eleven. These the hoes we don't want since they got their own money," Mann explained. "Free hoes fuck quicker!"

"True." Fresh agreed and nodded. It was true to a degree since most women who worked and took care of themselves tended to be a little more selective. The ones asking for drinks, weed and waffles were quicker to fuck.

Carlos felt a conflict from what he came from to what he come to believe. He grew up loving the profanity laden music blaring through the sound system but gave it up as a

Muslim. While some Muslims debated if music was permissible or not he just chose to abstain. Not only could he do without the negative, misogynistic lyrics he just found better use of his time.

Now he enjoyed the melodic recitation of the Qur'an. That didn't stop his head from nodding to the funky beat. Didn't stop him from posting up at a table with another cold beer in his hand or from accepting the next blunt in rotation.

"I heard ole Herman was down there with you? He said he was knocking niggas off?" Mann questioned. A dude from the neighborhood just returned from doing a bid as well and had war stories. According to him he was a cross between a bear and gorilla while in prison.

"Is that what he said?" Carlos laughed. It was pretty funny since Herman was in prison getting niggas off instead. He probably was gay before he went to prison but being around all those men brought it out.

"He said you was running with the Moozlimz too!" Fresh asked, cocking his head as if it was a dare.

"Is that what he said?" he repeated. He wasn't necessarily embarrassed about his faith, he just knew they wouldn't understand. That's why he would just hang out with them tonight and go to the masjid tomorrow. Hang out and turn up tonight and be righteous in the morning.

"I heard it's crazy down that road!" Hot Rod said with an audible timbre of fear in his voice. He had absolutely no business in the streets doing street shit because he was terrified of going to jail. The exact trait that makes dudes tell on everyone and everything they know when they get pinched. His own mother was in trouble for her tax schemes if he ever got knocked because he was going to tell on her too.

"Yeah," Carlos sighed and drifted back to that first day in prison. Seeing weak and white plucked away off the bat.

Hearing the screams from beatings, stabbings and rapes echoing in the night. Seeing the empty eyes of a rape victim the next morning. One white boy from middle Georgia caught a couple of years for breaking in houses. All he wanted was some new video games but ended up being passed around like a blunt. He chose swinging from the end of a bed rather than another night of that. He already hated black men but he really hated being raped by them.

"Is that Lil Los?" a scantily dressed hood rat asked as she led a flock of rats up to the table.

"Sup Ki-Ki" he replied and stood so she could hug him.

"That's right, my nigga fresh out the joint. One of y'all hoes need to go on and break him off!" Mann almost demanded like he was in charge of their vaginas. They were community coochie and belonged to all.

"Been wanting to fuck him!" a cute little 19 year old named Ally announced and stepped forward. Carlos remembered that illegal sexual intercourse was a big deal in Islam, but man, he been wanting to fuck her too. Maybe he could fuck her tonight, then take her to the masjid with him? He was going to need a wife so why not teach her Islam and clean her up like he was cleaned up.

"Uh oh!" Fresh cheered at the connection. He grabbed a rat for himself and hit the dance floor. Even if he didn't get laid at least he could get his grind on.

"Come on!" Ally demanded and pulled Carlos off his chair and onto the dance floor. She turned around and began bouncing her ass against his instant erection. It was foreplay in the hood.

Carlos let out another sigh and accepted his fate. He agreed with himself to drink, smoke and have sex with her then back to the deen in the morning. He'd missed all his prayers since getting out but would get back to it at dawn.

2:00 AM Saturday

Marlo lost the battle to stay awake and Freddy was right there waiting... *"Boy, why my door unlocked!" Marlo fussed when she pulled her burglar bar open without a key. Chances are no one would hit their house out of fear and respect for Thad and his mother in that order. Not the regular neighborhood thieves any way because crack heads don't discriminate between friend or foe, family or friends. They don't just burn bridges, they steal them and smoke them in their pipes.*

Marlo sucked her teeth and shook her head at the rumble of bass coming from his room. She rushed into her room and bathroom to relieve herself of the hour stuck in rush hour traffic.

"Whew!" she sighed, then let out a giggle at the loud sound of herself peeing. She saw a meme online stating that women with good pussy pee loud. She wiped, stood and washed her hands. She frowned curiously at her reflection and reflected. She knew something was amiss because her begging ass son hadn't coming begging for something.

He worked a little job and chipped in, but was like a child when it came to food. She decided what to eat for lunch each day with him in mind. She would only eat half of her food so she would stay fine and so he could eat the balance. He usually met her at the door but today he didn't come out of his room.

"Better not have that nasty girl in there!" she fussed and stomped down the hallway. She stopped short of busting in just in case he did have Dana in there again. "Thaddeus Johnson, you open this door right now!"

She banged on the door hurting her tiny hand but got no reply. She turned the knob and pushed the door open. The lingering smell of weed explained him laid out on the bed with his mouth open but didn't explain the blood. The coppery smell of blood permeated the air just beneath the weed.

"Thad?" she pleaded in contradiction to the large pool of blood

beneath his head. *She was more angry than sad and demanded her dead son to "Get up, this instant! You ain't even lock the burglar bars!"*

Thaddeus was silent, as dead people tend to be. Even when she shook his, foot, leg, then climbed on top of him in a futile attempt to wake the dead. A feat that hasn't been pulled off since Jesus by the will of his Lord.

"No baby! Noooooo!" she wailed and woke John beside her.

"What's wrong, baby?" he said even though he already knew. She had nightmares on a regular basis. So regular he began spending the night a lot less often.

"Yeah, I'm sorry. He was laughing at me! Laughing at Thaddeus!" she pouted and whined with her lip poked out.

"No, he's not. This is crazy. You gotta let it go, Marlo. How long you gonna torture yourself? Huh?" he asked insensitively while rubbing her sensitive vagina.

Marlo was too stunned by the question to reply. Out loud anyway because internally she was spewing a profanity laced tirade. She would never let it go. No, not ever.

She let out a frustrated sigh as he mounted her and pushed inside. She watched the ceiling fan rock in unison with his short, choppy stroke. He didn't bother to kiss or caress, just hump and grunt. Marlo felt lower than any other point ever in her life. They weren't in a relationship, yet he was inside of her raw as if they were. He reminded her of that fact with a final grunt and pulled out to ejaculate on her stomach.

"Mm, shit!" he gasped and rolled off. Seconds later he was snoring once again and once again she was alone in her pain.

"Let it go?" she huffed, shaking her head and breaking up with him in her head.

5:30 AM

"That nigga drunk!" Mann cheered happily as Carlos

stumbled from the club with his arm wrapped around Ally. No one he knew got a college degree or promotion at work so being pissy drunk was something to be celebrated.

Carlos was pretty drunk but the orange predawn glow still registered. It was time to pray but he was in no condition to stand before his Lord. He let out a sigh at missing yet another prayer and the sins still to be committed once they reached the rundown motel.

The four couples pushed the older Caprice to its limit when they piled inside. The kisses and gropes continued as Mann bent a few corners to the motel. Four couples equaled two double rooms for the group low on cash, morals and shame. Fresh and a girl whose name he didn't get, accompanied Carlos and Ally while Fresh, Mann and the other two girls got the other.

"Men are the protectors and maintainers of women," Carlos thought to himself as he watched Ally and the girl with no name take off their clothes. The strip show was over in seconds since neither wore much clothing to begin with.

"What you doing my nigga?" Fresh demanded when he saw Carlos didn't budge. His lowers desires battled with his belief and new found morals. He almost wanted to cry when his base self beat his higher self and helped him undress. Two years without a woman was more than he could stand. The devil whispered that Allah forgives again and again causing him to nod in agreement. He still planned to get right today, just a little detour inside the girl.

"I ain't got no rubber," he said thankful for a valid excuse not to enter the forbidden vagina.

"You don't need no rubber cuz I'm already pregnant. Going to Grady next week to get it out of me," she explained without explaining just giving birth a few months ago. She reached down and placed him near the entrance of her body.

"Wow!" Carlos heard himself say when he practically fell to the bottom of her well. Her vagina had an open floorplan without any walls whatsoever.

"It's good?" Ally asked even though she really couldn't feel much. They called him Lil Los because of his short stature. That extended into his underwear as well with a penis proportional to his height, aka short.

"Mmhm," he replied truthfully. It probably would have been a lot better with walls but two years is a long time. So long Carlos realized that he could do without it. Pussy cost him more than he could ever get back. His friend, big brother and mentor all in one. "Damn it!"

"I know!" Ally giggled taking it as a compliment. A few humps and pumps later Carlos began to moan. He went rigid and released pent up sexual frustrations. With that out the way he could go back to being righteous again. As soon as he woke up that is because a good nut will put a man to sleep quicker than Thanksgiving dinner. Ally had nowhere to go no time soon and fell asleep as well.

Fresh and his date screwed ten minutes longer and joined the snoring contest already in progress. Checkout time wasn't until 11:00 AM giving them all a much needed rest.

6:00 AM

"Un uh," Marlo declined when John tried to roll over on top and inside of her. He often got a quick nut before jumping in the shower to head to work.

"You sure?" he proposed while tapping his thick erection, on her thigh.

"I think my period coming," she lied to turn him off.

"I'll take a little head then," he offered as a consolation. The only thing she sucked was her teeth before she rolled off the bed. She went into her bathroom and sat on the toilet to pee. He stomped by and hopped in the shower complaining and grumbling. She made sure to flush so the rush of hot water would give him something to complain about.

He came out the bathroom completely naked as if to show her what she was missing out on. She agreed as she stole glance at his dangling meat but was done with him. His words that she *'get over it'* put a snarl on her face while she watched him.

"Too late now! I tried to give you some!" he laughed seeing her fixated on his dick. He pulled his boxers up as if punishing her. "I may, may swing through at lunch and give you a little. Maybe."

"Don't do me no favors. Matter fact, come through at lunch so you can get your shit. This..." she said pointing her finger back and forth between the two of them, "is over with."

"You tripping," he said, twisting his lips in disbelief. He finished dressing and headed to the door. He knew he would have to swing back during lunch with food and dick to fix whatever was wrong with her.

7:30 AM

Deputy Jenkins was too arrogant to be alarmed when all talking came to an abrupt halt when he walked into the briefing room. He tilted his head a little higher in pride since his coworkers were obviously in awe of him. He'd had meaningless sex with the three female deputies, even though only one of them actually looked like a female. Still, the other two had vaginas so he'd went in.

He could feel the stares and whispers while sipping his coffee. The captain walked in to start the briefing as he sipped his coffee. He didn't think much of the man and planned not to even listen to him. Instead he watched replays of his record setting day the day before on his phone.

"Excuse me, Deputy Jenkins? I hate to interrupt whatever

it is that you're doing," the captain said with a hint of sarcasm.

"I'm listening, Cap," he said without looking up. Had he looked up he would have seen two other deputies flanking him ready to pounce.

"Well, hear this." he said with a smile. It was an honor to arrest the pretty, playboy who bedded his department crush. "You're under arrest! Get him out of here!"

"What! Quit playing! Get off me!" he demanded while his coworkers clapped and cheered. He bitched and moaned while they dragged him away. So much for breaking his own record today.

11:05 AM

"A'ight my nigga!" Fresh shouted at the incessant knocking on the door. The maid was eager to change the nasty beds so she could go home. "Say Los, get up shawty, time to push."

Carlos frowned up at his friend trying to place the place he woke up in. He glanced at the sleeping girl next to him with a line of drool forming a pool on her pillow. Fresh held his finger to his mouth to shush his friend so he wouldn't wake the girls.

He knew it wasn't right but still eased out of the bed and quietly put his clothes back on. The two eased out of the room as Mann and Hot Rod did the same. It was their standard M.O to leave thots sleeping in motel rooms. The four friends climbed back in the car to make their escape.

"He hit?" Mann asked Fresh as he pulled from the parking lot.

"Fo about, two minutes!" he cracked up and rolled the next blunt up.

"After two years I'm surprised he lasted that long!" Hot Rod tossed in.

"'Shit, it's been longer than two years since he wasn't getting much ass 'fo he got locked up!" Mann cracked.

"Yeah, I was, I was smashing Dana!" Carlos shot back in his own defense and regretted it instantly. The car went quiet except for the engine knocking and bad CV joints clicking when he turned.

Everyone present knew that whatever had happened between him and Thad had something to do with Dana. Everyone present had also smashed Dana at least once since Carlos went away. One of them could possibly be her youngest child's daddy but so could a number of other men.

The blunt passed around the silence as they rode back to their hood. Mann made a quick detour to the local liquor store. Carlos shook his head at the thought of more alcohol but the blunt he smoked assured him it would be okay. *"I'll just hang out with his friends over the weekend, then Monday, I'ma get back on my deen,"* he told himself. It sounded reasonable so he nodded in agreement as Mann came out with several cases of beer. He got back behind the wheel and pulled out into traffic.

11:41 AM

Marlo almost grabbed her pistol in conjunction with the knocking on her burglar door since she wasn't expecting company. It was in her purse on top of her keys. The local burglars always knock before kicking the door in. She heard the small voice in his sing song tone and went to open it for her grandson.

"Hey, Miss Marlo. Donquatashawn wanted to see you. Been talkin' bout his granny all morning!" she lied as Marlo scooped the giggling boy into a firm grandma hug.

"Is that right Don-q, um, baby?" she asked failing to get the name right for once. She knew the little rat was lying since she was dressed slightly more slutty than normal. The tiny halter top showed slight stretch marks and nipples. An equally small pair of shorts displayed her wrinkled stomach and camel toe. "Did you bring a bag?"

"Of what?" the piss poor mother asked for the second time today. Her own mother had asked about a bag for her newborn when she left her home with her.

"Nothing," Marlo said since it would be easier to run out and grab whatever the toddler needed than trying to explain. Not to mention it gave her a chance to get out and show off her grandson. That sure beat moping around the house mourning her child all over again. Seeing Carlos again ripped the scabs off her heart just as they finally began to form. It's impossible to heal if the scab keeps coming off.

"Guess, you not coming to the cookout huh?" Dana asked scrunching her face up and shaking her head. "Probably not."

Marlo was about to ask what cookout since she loved a good cookout. She wouldn't eat just anyone's potato salad but loved her some ribs. She tilted her head upward and got the answer for herself from the activity across the street.

"Carlos home," she explained with a faux sad face. Little, however his name was pronounced, presence prevented Marlo from jumping on the girl. The thought of not being able to see her son's twin would literally kill her. She had no one else to love or love her back.

"I see," she said as Mann pulled the bucket to a squealing stop in front of the house. She missed whatever it was the girl said before she twisted her nasty little ass across the street. A cold chill of hate ran up her spine when she watched her grandson's mother embrace her son's killer.

"Why you ain't tell me when you was coming home?" Dana purred and gave him a squeeze. His face morphed into a question mark as he pondered the question. Taking responsibility for the 'incident' was one thing but it was still her fault. He had no intention on ever dealing with the girl again. She did look good though.

"Um," was the best he could come up with. She did feel good though so he squeezed her back. No telling how long they would have stood there hugging but he broke it off when he saw Miss Marlo giving him the evil eye from across the street. "Come on. Let's go 'round back."

If looks could kill the two would have dropped dead on the spot as she shot daggers into their backs. They received the opposite reaction when they reached the backyard.

"There go my baby!" Nita cheered and jumped up from her lawn chair. Her 40 year-old body jiggled in the age inappropriate clothing she'd selected. Even her son zoomed in on the bouncing breast then quickly turned away since they were his mother's bouncing breast.

"Hey, Mama," he replied feeling embarrassed by her appearance. Her outfit was almost the same as Dana's just in a different color. Her shorts were pulled up tightly to show off her vagina and her nipples pressed through her halter top as well. He vowed to call his mother to Islam when he came home but, here she was passing him a blunt.

"Smoke something!" she cheered and danced. This wasn't the time nor place to preach so he accepted it and took a pull. "See you got lil mama with you. She been checking on you the whole time you been gone!"

"Mmhm," Dana nodded proudly. All she did was ask 'how Los' whenever she saw her coming or going. Most of the time she was with yet another dude.

"You wanna fix him a burger? The ribs ain't going on til later," Nita asked so she could finally have a moment with her son. Dana almost turned her nose up at the notion of serving a man but caught on and agreed. She wasn't going to fix his food but would give them some space.

"Sup mama?" Carlos asked since he caught it too. Especially since Dana just walked over to the next blunt in rotation and slid in.

"You," she smiled and looked her son over. He had definitely matured in the two years he'd been gone. What she couldn't see was the internal changes he'd made. His heart was no longer black but every missed prayer, toke of smoke, sip of beer and touch of a woman added a stain on his heart. It would grow black with every sin until completely black and dead.

"Have you seen Miss Marlo?" Nita sighed. "You know we ain't talked since, you know."

"Naw, I ain't seen her yet," he almost lied. He had seen her but didn't look at her. He knew he had to face her one day. As part of his repentance he needed to apologize.

"You need to talk to her. You done told me you sorry 'bout what happened but did you tell her? That's who you need to say sorry to. She lost her child. I know I ain't the best mama in the world but I would lay down and die if something happened to you. I cain't even look her in her face no more!"

"Don't cry, Mama," he pleaded seeing a lone tear stream down her face. "I'ma go over there and talk to her. Tomorrow, okay?"

"Okay, baby. Make sure you do," she agreed and knocked the tear away. "You ready to eat?"

"I need to hop in the shower first," he said since he could still smell Ally on him. His mother admired his growth as he walked into the house.

1:00 PM

"You just like your daddy!" Marlo giggled at her grandson. It was uncanny how much the child was like his father. He had all of his mannerisms even though they would never meet. Even Thaddeus's father popped in and out but he would never get to see him.

"Dada," the child repeated as if he knew he was supposed to have one.

"Dada," she repeated, using everything she had not to cry. It was deja vu when her grandson pointed at the toy store as they walked through the mall. "Want a toy?"

The child nodded and pointed as she led him inside to pick out whatever he wanted. She was unable to prevent the tears from falling when he picked out a truck just like his father used to do. She got herself together by the time she met Janice in the food court.

"Hey, girl. Is this your grand baby?" Janice cooed and scooped the toddler off his feet. He looked to his grandmother curiously since he wasn't accustomed to affection.

"Yes, that's little, um, Thaddeus," she decided. His real name was too much for her so she would call him Thad from now on.

"Well, hello there Mr. Thad," she sang and sat him down. "S and S?"

"Sure! I could go for a pizza stuffed burger with a heap of parmesan fries!" she said taking a break from her diet.

"Uh oh! Not you eating a stuffed burger! You sure you don't want no black bean burger? Or veggie?" Janice dared. She was a proud big girl with no need to diet since men love big fine just as much as they love slim fine.

"Nah, I'm trying to get fine like you so I can find myself a new man," she said breaking the news of the breakup.

"A new one! What's wrong with the one you got?" she reeled in disbelief.

"Wrong? What's right with him! Just sick of him! Ugh!" she grunted and shivered.

"Good cuz he kept trying holla at me! Every time I been around y'all he wink anytime you blink," Janice admitted.

"I seen him. Saw you frown up at him too. Most times women would giggle or wink back. I'm glad you kept it real," Marlo replied.

"One, cuz I'm your friend for real. And two that's just nasty! That thang between his legs gonna get him in trouble one day," she said unknowing today was that day.

"Chile, that's the only thing I'm going to miss about him," she laughed honestly. He was plenty handsome but wore a smug look that made him ugly. She shivered once more at the thought of him.

1:30 PM

"I can't eat this. This is what we feed the inmates!" Jenkins fussed when a tray was slid into his cell. All deputies have to start out at the jail so he knew he would be held in protective custody away from the other inmates. He also knew how bad the jail food was since it was, jail food. He always wondered how people survived on it for weeks, months and years. He was about to find out since he was charged with sodomy and other serious sex related crimes.

"And you are an inmate!" a female deputy shot back with malice on her breath. She shoved the tray inside the slot so viciously the beans sloshed into the applesauce.

"Hey!" he griped since he was going to eat the sauce but not the beans. "What is your problem?"

"You!" she shot back and stormed off. Her angry strides made her large ass shift catching the womanizer's eye. He was about to think how she looked like she had some good-good, wet-wet until he remembered she did.

"Oh yeah!" he chuckled as he recalled hitting her from the back then sneaking out when she went to sleep. She didn't take kindly to being hit and quit. It was ten years ago but it still stung. He may be laughing but actually the joke was on him since she was going home at the end her shift. He was already at home where he would be for a long time to come.

Coercing the daughter of two prominent lawyers to blow him to avoid arrest was going to cost him. Her gags and crying during the blow jog could be clearly heard on the surveillance footage. So was her breaking down in heaving sobs after he left.

1:45 PM

Carlos literally had to force himself out of the shower. It was the most peace and privacy he had to shower in years, even with a full-fledged party going on in the backyard. Not to mention being able to adjust the water just how he wanted it. In prison you got what they gave you. Either too hot or too cold.

"Shit! I mean shoot!" he corrected since the new Carlos aka Hasan didn't curse much. He still hated having to deal with his old friends and old life even if it was just for one more day. "Going to the masjid tomorrow!"

Carlos dressed in his new clothes while regretting his decision to come home. He should have paroled out to his grandmother's house where he didn't know any one. Where no one knew him and he could be whoever he wanted to be. Namely Hasan Muwakil, the Muslim. Because everyone was waiting on Lil Los to come back outside to drink, smoke and turn up. He wanted to turn them down but felt like he owed them. He would repay that debt today then get back on the straight path tomorrow. He nodded in agreement to his plan but still forgot to say In sha Allah.

"Here he go! Come dance with yo' mama!" Nita cheered when her son emerged from the house. The size of the party had doubled in size so she wanted a little attention before his friends swooped him away.

"Okay," he said with a defeated sigh. Seeing his mother dressed and dancing like a teen scraped against his soul. She was twerking and popping and dropping just like the younger thots. After all the only difference between a young thot and an old thot is twenty years and perhaps some vaginal elasticity.

"Uh oh. Uh oh!" Nita cheered and shook. Shook and twerked along with her son to the latest jam coming through the speakers. It didn't take long until the rhythm hit him and he did the dances from two years ago. Jail is like a time machine, so to him it was still 2015 when he went away.

4:45 PM

"Hmp" Marlo huffed when she pulled onto her street and saw not only had the party not ended it had actually grown. She contained her protest to her own mind since she had her grandson with her. She knew she could keep him as long as there was a party going on. There was always a party going on somewhere which made her think about keeping him fulltime.

Dana certainly wouldn't mind since that would free her up to sling her public privates all over the city. She would too but tonight they belonged to Carlos. His friends wouldn't mind since they had it for the two years he'd been gone.

Her grandson had fallen asleep from the movement of the car so she unstrapped him from his car seat and carried him to the door. It was a little tricky trying to open the burglar bar and front doors holding the child. Luckily, she had plenty of practice from decades of shopping sprees. Once inside she laid the toddler down on the sofa and went back for his new clothes and toys from the car. Both would be staying there since the ratchet girl's house was the Bermuda Triangle for new shit. Everything she ever sent over there came up missing.

"Whaaat?" Marlo laughed upon hearing her seldom used home phone ring. She so rarely used it she had to check her contacts to give someone the number. For that reason she let it ring and continued what she was doing. Her curiosity was sparked by the third time it rung prompting her to pick up. "Hello?"

"You have a collect call from an inmate at the Fulton County Jail, 'John Jenkins', to accept press one. To decline press two. To block..."

"Hello?" Marlo asked with the same curiosity that made her answer.

"Thank God! I've been calling you all day! Where the hell you been?" John demanded like he was in a position to make demands. He hadn't got the memo yet but they were broken up.

"Um..." Marlo said in confusion. She had been confused as to why he would be calling collect from jail but his demands really threw her for a loop. "Not that I answer to you but, I took my grandson to the mall. I hope that's to your liking?"

"I guess. Look I got arrested for some bull shit. I won't be able to see a judge until Monday. Make sure you're there with your deed to make my bond," he ordered. That too was pretty confusion to Marlo.

"Um..." she repeated since she couldn't find the words she was looking for. A moment later they came to her brain and rushed out of her mouth. "Just why would I do that? I'm not dealing with you ever again. Whenever you work out whatever you got going on, your stuff is packed right by the front door."

"Listen, bitch, I have some serious shit going on. Don't fucking play with me! Trust me, you don't want to get on my bad side!"

"Fuck both sides, bottom, top, um, middle! I got something for your ass you come around here!" Marlo said, looking towards the sofa table near the front door. On it was her purse, in it was her pistol.

"Bit...shit!" he fussed when she hung up. He called right back and got no answer. Marlo did listen to the complete instructions this time so he was blocked the next time he called. "Bitch!"

10:30 PM

"Me and Jose finna go to the movies," Nita announced as the party began to wind down. After a day of eating, smoking and drinking it was time for most people to hit the club.

"We are?" Jose asked with a confused frown. He'd invited her home for sex and didn't know anything about any movies. He wasn't quite swift enough to catch the woman might not want to tell her son that. She looked at him and shook her head. If he hadn't had such good weed she might have changed her mind.

"Plus, I know you and lil bit want to be alone," she said with a wink that made Dana giggle and snuggle up against him.

"Oh," Carlos replied since he really didn't want to be alone with the girl. Once again he let out a sigh and gave in to what everyone else wanted. "Okay."

Nita left with her other boyfriend leaving the two in the midst of an awkward silence. Not breaks the ice like a good shot of pussy so Dana offered him one.

"Let's go to your room," she said and got up to lead the way. He recalled the good times and good sex they'd had in that room as he got up. He looked down at her ass and noticed it was wider and fatter than when he left. Two years of back shots and a second child will do that.

It was just like old times when Dana immediately began

to strip as soon as they got to the room. It was just like new times when Carlos followed and stripped out of his clothes as well. Dana climbed on the bed and spread her legs. Carlos caught a slight whiff of the sex she'd had earlier but he had an erection and overlooked it.

"You miss this good pussy, huh?" she asked hopefully as he climbed between her legs and rolled a condom on.

"Um, yeah," he replied preparing to enter. It didn't take much prep since she was slippery wet and loose. He noticed it was nothing like he remembered but she was a good actor and moaned and groaned, thrashed like he was killing it.

Two years is a long time and vagina is vagina so it didn't take long for him to get fully involved. He lifted her legs folded her into 'the buck'. The room filled with the sounds and smell of rough sex. Yeah, two years is a long time and he did great to last more than two minutes.

"Argh! Shit! Whew! Mmm" he said while going through convulsions and spasms of orgasm.

"It was good?" she pleaded. Dana hadn't finished high school but was smart enough to understand her only strength lay between her legs. The plump mound of flesh was all she had to offer a man.

"Yeah," he responded because it had been two years. A lot had changed in that time besides the size of her vagina. He wanted to drift into his thoughts but her incessant chatter wouldn't allow it. He nodded and 'mmhm-ed' along to whatever she was talking about until something registered. He sat straight up and asked "What you just say?"

"Huh?" she asked since she wasn't quite sure herself. Even she knew she had the tendency to rattle absentmindedly just to fill the space. "Oh, about Thaddeus? Just wish he could see his son grow up. I wish y'all ain't fall out."

"I wish we didn't either. I wish he never started dissing

me. We were 'sposed to be boys," Carlos said meaning every syllable. The pain was evident in his voice but it was about to get worse. Turn up, like they say.

"Thad? Talking shit about you? Boy, stop! He loved you! Said you was his lil brother!" She sat up and declared. "Who told you he was talking shit about you? They a damn lie!"

Carlos strained his face and memory and clearly recalled the conversation that led to the incident. Right here in this same bed, naked after sex. He let it replay in his head and it made even less sense now than it did then. He found it hard to believe but had been persuaded by the power of the pussy. Victorious vaginas had vanquished better men than he since the beginning of time.

"Get out," he said so softly it didn't sound like the command that it was. So softly she wasn't sure if she heard what she thought she heard.

"Huh?" she asked since 'excuse me' wasn't a part of her limited vocabulary. She just knew he didn't tell her to get out after he got off, like so many other men had.

"Get dressed, and get out," he repeated just as calmly. The realization that he'd killed his friend for nothing squeezed his chest and made breathing difficult.

"You just want yo' dick sucked!" she said twisting her lips. She dipped her head to give him some head but he pushed her away.

"No, I just want you to go and never come back. Don't ever come near me or my mama again!" he insisted.

"Fuck you and yo mama!" she shot back and leaped from the bed. She cursed them both as she scrambled to get dressed. She couldn't locate her panties from flinging them somewhere and dressed without them. Luckily they came five to a pack because she ran through them on a regular.

Carlos had secretly shed many a tear since the incident

but never like the chest heaving, snot out the nose bawling he did now. His heart wrenching wails could be heard all throughout the empty house.

The crying stopped just as suddenly as it began when he realized what needed to be done. He wiped his face with his hands and put his clothes back on. He slid his new tennis shoes over his bare feet and left his room. He stepped out on the front porch and looked across the street. The darkness of Marlo's house was the only thing that prevented him from walking over there and giving her the apology she deserved. The one she desperately needed to heal. She would have thanked him for it and for saving her from another nightmare of finding her dead son.

"Tomorrow," he sighed and went back inside the house. Again he forgot to say In sha Allah since tomorrow isn't promised to anyone. And despite your best efforts, you cannot will unless God wills.

1:30 AM Sunday

"Shit!" Carlos muttered when another deep yawn shook his body. He knew what fate awaited him when he went to sleep. He knew it was the devil and not Freddie waiting to give him another bad dream.

He smoked more weed hoping to either stay awake or fall so deeply asleep he could hide from the devil. Not happening because the only refuge from the devil is with God. People who turn to people or intoxicants only compound their problems. There is no reward for good except good, so what about sin. All good is from God, whatever bad happens is from our own hands.

He let out a defeated sigh as drifted off to sleep...

"Called me lame!" Carlos fumed as he exhaled a plume of weed smoke. Meanwhile Shaiton whispered sinister suggestions into his ear like sweet nothings. The devil's job is to make wicked deeds

seem fair. That's why he grabbed his gun to go check his friend, mentor and surrogate big brother.

Carols stepped off his porch and marched across the street. They were close enough to have an open door policy but today he knocked since this was a formal visit.

"Who?" Thaddeus called from inside his room. Working nights allowed him to sleep during the day but having the house to himself allowed him to have girls over and gone before his mama came home. He laughed to himself thinking about his mother sniffing the air for scents of sex when she came in. She was the proud owner of a clean, well maintained vagina and could smell the opposite from a mile away.

"Shit!" he fussed when the knocking continued and he realized he would have to get out of bed. Hopefully whoever it was had a vagina to make up for being inconvenienced. "Los? Why you knocking on the door?"

Thaddeus pushed the burglar door latch and it came right open since he never locked it when he was home. His mother was a lot more cautious and kept it locked when she was home. She kept her keys right on top of her pistol in her purse near the front door. He teased her about that all the time knowing she wouldn't bust a grape let alone a burglar.

"Cuz, I need to..." his big speech was put on pause when Thad began walking back to his room to lay back down. He felt even more disrespected as followed to make his point. "Yeah, like I was saying. I heard you was talking shit about me!"

"Probably was," Thaddeus chuckled as he plopped down on his bed. "Let me guess, Dana told you this huh?"

"Yeah!" he shot back. In his mind it was proof that she was telling the truth. Truth was Thaddeus knew she was a trouble maker and expected it when he saw his partner hook up with her. "Said you said I was lame!"

"Shit, you is if you believe anything that bitch say. You know she running around saying she pregnant for me," he sighed.

"Nigga you lame!" he shot back and pulled the pistol to prove it. Thaddeus began to laugh hysterically at his friend holding the gun in his shaking hand. The laughter stung so much he pulled the hammer back cocking the gun. "You think it's a game?"

"Yes," Thaddeus laughed as his friend struggled to hold the large gun in his small hand. He adjusted his grip putting a hair too much pressure on its hair trigger. The gun sounded like a cannon blast when it went off in the small room.

"Oh shit! My bad!" he frantically apologized. He just knew big brother was about to beat him up for shooting the gun in his room. Probably would have if not for the strange look in his eye. That far away, unfocused gaze of the dead. "Thad? Thad! Oh shit!"

Carlos grabbed the phone to call 9-1-1 but realized his friend was gone. He quickly hung up because it was he who'd sent him wherever it was he went. His DNA and prints were on the phone when he sat it down. He ran around the house in a panic trying to figure out his next move. The best he could come up with was to go home and pretend like nothing happened. He would just play dumb when asked if he saw or heard anything. There was no witnesses so no one could say what happened one way or the other.

"Where Thad at?" Mann asked as he and Fresh smoked with Carlos on the porch a few hours later. They couldn't go inside since Nita always wanted to hit the weed. Not to mention she never wore enough clothes and it bothered him seeing his friends looking at her tits and ass.

"I'on know?" Carlos said sounding so phony even he frowned along with his friends. None of them thought much so none of them thought anything about it. The weed rotated in conjunction with inane conversation about rappers, actors and chicks with fat asses.

"That's who I wanna fuck," Mann admitted when they watched

Marlo turn on the street. Carlos began to hold his breath at that point. "Don't tell Thad I said that!"

"She is fine though!" Fresh cosigned when Marlo stepped out of her car wearing a snug business suit skirt and blouse. Her panty's lines where visible from across the street and all eyes tuned in.

"Hey, Carlos, fellas!" she smiled and waved at the boys before turning to go inside. The round ass shifted side to side as she climbed the stairs. She let out a little chuckle knowing the boys were looking at her backside.

Carlos tried to hold his breath but realized he already had been holding it. He let it out and traded it for another. He braced himself for the outburst but it didn't come. Not yet anyway since Marlo rushed straight to the bathroom to relieve herself. She had been telling herself for the last fifteen minutes of her commute that fly girls don't pee on themselves. She barely made it and got to keep her fly girl status.

"Hmp?" Carlos grunted to himself. He just realized that the whole thing didn't even happen. It was just a bad dream he had from smoking to much weed. He shook his head and began to laugh at himself. "I'm tripping."

"About what?" Mann asked but before he could answer Marlo busted out her door hysterically.

"Help! Someone shot my baby!" she pleaded. The sound of her screams shook his very soul and sent a shiver up his spine. He could hear that scream to this day as vividly as he did that day. To make matters worse she ran straight across the street to him. "Help me, Carlos! We gotta wake him up!"

"I don't, um, ain't see..." he explained as she hugged him tightly. The scream echoed again and woke him again as it had many nights since it happened...

7:00 AM

"Shit!" Carlos fussed when the bad dream snatched him from a fitful sleep. He let out a sigh seeing he had missed his dawn prayer once again. He thought about making ablution to pray but felt the effects of all the weed he smoked. The ritual purification doesn't clean away intoxicants since they are forbidden in the first place. Not to mention he was in a state of sexual impurity from the nasty girl. Muslims must bathe between sex and prayer, but that's for married people. He wondered if there was an injunction for sex with thots.

"Shit!" he repeated since this was the day he was supposed to get it together. To get back on his deen, but it was starting out on the wrong foot once again. Being a Muslim is not just what you do, it's who you are. Every second, every breath, worshipping your Lord who created you.

"Carlos! You home?" Nita called out as she came through the door. Jose proved once again that he was no gentleman and pulled off before she even reached the front door. He made his point last night and again this morning with rough sex.

"In here!" he called out and went to her in the living room. Nita looked just like she had been sexed all night. She had bags under her eyes and her hair was all over her head. She winced with pain from her battered vagina when she plopped down on the sofa. "Sup, Mama."

"You!" said smiling at her handsome son. She made a big production as she produced the neatly rolled blunt she swiped from Jose's ashtray. She reasoned it wasn't technically stealing since she had his semen swimming around in her. "Fire it up!"

"Un uh, I ain't smoking no more!" he firmly declined and went on to explain. "I'm Muslim now. I took my Shahadah in prison. I ain't 'sposed smoke or drink or have sex..."

"Muslims cain't have sex!" she reeled. "It's bad enough

you cain't eat no pork skins but cain't fuck! See, that's why I couldn't be no moozlim!"

"Muslim, and yeah we can fu...have sex. Just gotta be married. I been smoking and drinking just to be thankful for err body coming to see me and holding me down but I gotta get right. Get to the masjid..." he explained leaving out the part about crossing the street to apologize and beg for forgiveness.

"So, you smoke with yo' friends but not with yo' mama? I'm the one carried you in my belly. It was me who pushed yo' big head out they pussy! I'm the one..."

"Okay, Nama! Last one! No more after this! After this I'm getting back on my deen!" he insisted. None of that meant much to Nita who was just happy to get her way. She gloated internally as her son lit the weed and took a pull.

"So, since you a moozlim now you gonna be blowing yo'self up and running people down in trucks?" she asked sincerely since that's all she saw about Muslims. For whatever reason media exclusively shows atrocities committed by so-called Muslims but never the good.

"Mama, that stuff ain't got nothing to with Islam! Matter fact, all that stuff is forbidden in Islam!" he defended. "Allah and our prophet Muhammad, peace be upon him, never told us to do that. They both commanded us to do good on the earth. He, The Most High, set it in order, it's not for us to spoil that."

"So, why women gotta walk behind men?" she wanted to know. Carlos did too since that too had nothing to do with Islam.

"Beats me," he shrugged. "See, sometimes people from other places mix Islam with whatever they culture is. They making they own religion when they do that, cuz that ain't Islam. Our prophet Muhammad, peace be upon him said he was *only sent to perfect good manners*. So anytime you see anything else just know that ain't Islam!"

"So, why women gotta wear all them clothes? They be looking all hot!"

"Not as hot as hell fire, but still, it's to protect women. Men are supposed to be the protectors and maintainers of women. Not exploit and use them. Women dress like that cuz that's what men want. If men stepped up and be men and tell women not to dress like prostitutes they wouldn't do it!"

"Well, I don't dress like no prostitute!" she shot back.

"Yes, you do, Mama, but that's my fault cuz I allowed it," he explained.

"You ain't allow me to do nothing, I'm grown!" she shot back. "Shoot, I'm the one pay all the bills around here! When you start paying them then you can tell me what to wear!"

"That's a bet cuz that's exactly what I'm finna do. You trust me right? You know I wouldn't tell you nothing bad right?" he challenged.

"Yeah, I trust you," she said softly. Everything he was saying made sense so why wouldn't she. The blunt found its way into a mayonnaise top turned ashtray and smoldered out as they talked. They talked for hours as he tried to answer all of her questions while explaining Islam's number one tenant.

"There's nothing worthy of worship except for God, who create us. That's the first commandment ain't it?" he challenged.

"Yes," she agreed since she still knew the ten by heart from church as a child. She had broken many of them and it never bothered her until that moment. A tear fell from her eye when she realized just how far she strayed from those commandments. "Can I go with you down to that temple?"

"Muslims don't have no temples mama!" he laughed.

"That's the nation of Islam and they ain't got nothing to do with Islam. All that white man is the devil bullshit!"

"Yeah cuz ain't none of these devils running around here white," she huffed indignantly at the crazy notion.

"Islam ain't black, white or Arab. It's about worshipping God and doing good deeds. Period. And yes you can come but..." he said frowning at her mini dress and half shirt.

"Prolly should change huh?" she giggled and stood. She held her head high and marched down the hall to her room.

Carlos had a night of sex too and went to take a shower of his own. An hour later they were clean, sober and ready to take a positive step in their lives. There's no reward for good except good and they were ready to do good.

12:57 PM

The mother and son stepped from the house to drive over to the masjid on 14th Street. He stopped in his tracks and looked across the street.

"I need to holla at Miss Marlo," he said nodding in agreement.

"Yeah, you do," his mother agreed. She pressed her lips together in a proud smile and hugged him tightly. They looked at each other and nodded once more in confirmation. She watched her grown son march across the street to do the right thing.

12:59 PM

"Better not be John!" Marlo growled in response to her ringing doorbell. She sat her grandson's lunch in front of him and went to the door. Her heart dropped when she saw Carlos standing at the door. She turned to her purse as he turned to get a reassuring nod from his mama.

1:00 PM

It was exactly 48 hours after being released that Marlo

opened her front door. She raised the pistol and shot him right between his eyes.

"Now, I'm over it."

THE END.

KEEP READING FOR FREE BONUS READ.

The following is Sa'id Salaam's ode to his favorite urban author. It is a concept book, not for sale.